The
Barons'
Hostage

GEOFFREY TREASE

THOMAS NELSON INC., PUBLISHERS
NASHVILLE   NEW YORK

All rights reserved under International and Pan-American Conventions. Published by Thomas Nelson Inc., Publishers, Nashville, Tennessee. Manufactured in the United States of America.

First U.S. edition

Library of Congress Cataloging in Publication Data

Trease, Geoffrey.
  The barons' hostage.

  SUMMARY: The lives of a teen-age boy laying claim to a barony and a teen-age girl whose marriage has been arranged by the King's adversary become closely entwined during the Barons' War in England.
    1. Montfort, Simon of, Earl of Leicester, 1208?–1265—Juvenile fiction. 2. Barons' war, 1263–1267—Juvenile fiction [1. Montfort, Simon of, Earl of Leicester, 1208?–1265—Fiction. 2. Barons' war, 1263–1267—Fiction. 3. Great Britain—History—13th century—Fiction] I. Title.
PZ7.T6895Bar5   [Fic]   75–11638
ISBN 0–8407–6434–0

CONTENTS

THE BARONS' HOSTAGE

1

A Horn in the Hills

IT WAS STRANGE. No, more than strange. Uncanny. Dinner was over, and, since there was nothing but a white clammy mist outside, blotting out the dale, the family had retired up the spiral stair to their private chamber over the hall. The younger ones—Margery, who was nine, and Robert, a year younger—were sprawled in front of the log fire. Michael was reciting what bits he could remember of the *Song of Roland*, filling in the gaps with his own words. Their mother had taken her carved, high-backed chair to the left of the fireplace, where she divided her attention between her embroidery, the baby, Blanche, crawling amid the rushes on the floor, and the story her elder son was telling.

They had just got to the thrilling part where Roland and the French rear guard are ambushed by the Moorish hordes in the high pass of Roncesvalles, and at last Roland blows his magic horn for help, so that the Emperor Charlemagne will ride back with the main body.

"Oh, *please* go on!" begged Margery.

"Well, he put the horn to his lips—it was all gold

and crystal, very beautiful—and he blew till the veins stood out on his temples. And the sound went stealing down the long mountain passes, out of Spain, into the fair land of France. And the old emperor heard it as he rode at the head of his host—thirty leagues away he was by then—"

"Thirty leagues!" echoed Robert, goggling.

"I said it was a magic horn," Michael pointed out severely. "It was faint and thin and ghostly, stealing on their ears out of the high mountains—"

It was then that the uncanny thing happened. Out of the hills, faint and thin and ghostly, came the long-drawn note of a horn.

For a moment they could not believe their ears. They were so deeply under the spell of the story that the horn seemed to come to them from a bygone age. Only when it was repeated did they jump to their feet and cram themselves into the alcove by the window.

"It's no good," said Margery, "you can't see a thing. The mist—"

"I'm going up on the roof!" cried Michael.

They thrust aside the tapestry in the corner of the room and clattered up the winding stairs. There was not much more to see when they reached the battlements. The whole dale was shrouded in mist. They could make out the roofs of the village toward the river—but there was no sign of the moors and crags beyond.

Old William, the watchman, came panting and grumbling up the other staircase. They turned to him eagerly.

"Whoever can it be? Not visitors?"

"Her ladyship isn't expecting no visitors—none that I know of, anyway, Master Robert. It'll just be some ordinary folk lost their way in the forest, I reckon. Mistook our dale for Mallowdale, most like, with this mist coming down, and now they're lost, and wondering how they'll get down by nightfall."

The horn rang out again. Michael stood like a hound with ears pricked. The old man was right. It was neither a hunting call nor the salutation of an approaching guest. It could only be meant as a distress signal.

"What are you going to do?" he demanded.

The watchman raised his own horn. "Gi' them a toot wi' this," he grunted. "Show them which way to head for—"

"Don't be such a fool," said Michael, horrified. "Do you realize where these people are?"

William looked offended. Neither his sight nor his hearing was quite what it had been, but so long as he had wind to blow his horn he meant to stay watchman of Hardraw Castle. It was not as though it were an important stronghold. Nothing had ever happened at Hardraw, or would.

"They're up in the forest somewhere, like I said, Master Michael," he answered sulkily.

The boy snorted. "Somewhere! They're up there." He pointed due north into the dirty-white haze. "That horn was blown just under Raven's Edge—you could tell by the way it echoed off the crags."

"Ar," said William, afraid to contradict but unwilling to agree.

"If you sound your horn they'll make straight in this direction—and you know what that means!"

11

"Ar. I follow you, Master Michael. They'll likely pitch headfirst down Walden Scar."

"They likely would," Michael answered mockingly. Even in clear sunlight the green hillside below the rocks of Raven's Edge was a deceptive place for strangers. It looked down over peaceful Hardraw, giving a bird's-eye view of the dale for miles—the winding river, the striped field, the village clustered grayly beneath the square tower of the castle. A lost traveler might be excused for hailing that vision with a shout of relief, and for starting headlong down the slope toward it. What he might not realize until too late was that the steep hillside of turf and bracken ended abruptly in an edge as clear-cut as the gutter of a house roof, and below it, for a hundred feet or more, the naked limestone cliff fell sheer as a wall to the river. Walden Scar was dangerous at any time. By night or in mist, it was a deathtrap.

Once again the strangers' horn wailed despairingly from the heights opposite.

"Couldn't we shout to them?" asked Margery.

"Just as bad," said Michael curtly. "They'd not hear the words, but they'd hear our voices and come this way."

"Oh, what *can* we do?"

"Go up and guide them down."

"Oh, can I come?" Robert inquired eagerly.

"No, you'd never keep up. I've got to get to them before they do anything silly." Michael turned toward the stairs when an idea struck him. "I'd better have something to signal with when I get up there, in case I can't find them. Lend me your horn, William."

"Nay, I can't part wi' this. I'm watchman of Hardraw, an' this horn o' mine—"

"Don't, then," snapped Michael. He ran down from the roof and burst into the chamber, calling explanations to his mother as he rummaged for his father's old hunting horn.

"Oh, be careful—" she began, but before she could say more he was hurtling down the lower stairs, through the great hall, and down into the courtyard.

There was a ford half a mile downstream, but Michael headed for a nearer place where it was possible to jump and scramble from one great tilted boulder to another. Now the gray precipice loomed over him. To the left a tongue of green slanted up one flank, like the steep ramp leading to a castle gateway. He knew what the mist above still concealed—that this green rift was the only shortcut to the heights where the lost travelers were still, at intervals, sending out their signals of distress. He toiled upward, gasping; the bracken was waist-high and beaded with wet.

Meanwhile, unaware of the hidden gulf at her feet, Arlette de la Garde was enjoying the excitement.

Most of her brief life since the death of her parents had been passed in a convent. It had not been a particularly strict convent. Ladies from the outside world had often stayed there, bringing their fine clothes and maids and lapdogs and gay gossip about the court. Even the nuns themselves had been continually in trouble with the bishop, what with their dancing and music, their forbidden luxuries at table,

13

and their stubborn refusal to keep the dress regulations. He had complained again only last year about their low necklines and jewelry. Still, convent life had been placid on the whole, especially for the schoolgirls. It had certainly not included getting lost in the wilds of Yorkshire.

There were four of them in the party: Sister Helena, tight-lipped and leather-faced, sitting her horse like a warrior, Adam and John, the two convent menservants, and she herself, Arlette. It was John who kept blowing his horn and listening for some answer. Adam brought up the rear, leading the packhorse with Arlette's small baggage.

"We should ha' gone the long road 'round, ma'am," said John with a mournful shake of the head.

"And lost a day?" retorted Sister Helena. "Nonsense, man. They said it was safe; we could not miss it."

"But we *have* missed it," Arlette pointed out.

"Not at all, child." The nun was strong-minded and of aristocratic birth. She was not accustomed to being wrong. "John has blundered a shade too far to the right—or it may be to the left—it is really of no consequence. We have only to go carefully forward and we can hardly fail to come down into Mallowdale. If only we could hit upon a stream, we should have no difficulty."

"Why, Sister Helena?"

"I have always understood that if you are lost in the hills—not that we *are* lost, but if one were, you understand—the safest thing is to follow running water until it leads you down into the valley."

"I can hear running water—down there." Arlette

pointed down the hillside which fell steeply, at the angle of a house roof, until it faded into the mist.

"Then we had better make for it. And perhaps it would be wise to lead the horses." The nun slid stiffly from the saddle. "John!" she called sharply. "Stop blowing that horn—it is obvious there is nobody for miles, or they would have answered by now. We are going down to the stream. You will have to dismount —there is no danger, but it is somewhat steep."

At that moment there was an answering blast from a horn behind them. John paused, and decided it was better to disobey orders. He raised his own horn, and once more the plaintive sound echoed thinly through the mist.

Arlette was already creeping down the slope, coaxing her horse behind her. She was not too happy about the descent herself. There was a suggestion of emptiness in front, as though nothing much lay behind the hanging curtains of the mist. The running water seemed so very far below. And she did not like the way her mare laid back her ears and dug her hooves in till the reins tautened.

"Stop!" cried a high, boyish voice.

Arlette stood and watched a youthful figure advancing from the mist. At first he was no more than a slender gray shadow, then she saw a dark, wine-red tunic and blue hose, a pink face almost aflame with exertion, and brown hair slashed across in a fringe, unkempt and glistening with moisture.

Sister Helena was still dragging her reluctant horse down the slope.

"Stop!" yelled the boy again, waving his arms. "Stop!"

15

The nun paused. "Are you addressing me, young man?" she demanded. Bishops' chaplains—even bishops themselves—had wilted at the tone. But to Arlette's secret delight, the young stranger seemed quite unimpressed.

"You don't want to break your neck, madam. There's a hundred-foot drop to the river, just there."

"Oh," said the nun with dignity, "in that case . . ." She began to lead her horse up the slope again.

Arlette, despite her convent upbringing, was quite competent to distinguish one boy from another. She moved toward the interesting newcomer without undue hesitation. In a minute or two Sister Helena would reach them and take control of the conversation.

"Where did *you* spring from?" she asked with a smile.

He pointed down into the unseen dale. "Hardraw. I'm Michael Vallier. It was very strange. I was telling my brother and sister about Roland's magic horn when we heard your man sounding his."

"Strange," she agreed, "and lucky for us."

"It's rather like *The Song of Roland*—up here, today, I mean," he jerked out awkwardly, and quoted:

" 'High are the hills and huge and dim with cloud—' "

Quick as lightning she capped the quotation:

" 'Down in the deeps, the living streams are loud.' "

He stared at her with a pleased expression in his brown eyes. "Fancy your knowing that!"

Her darker eyes twinkled. "I am not completely ignorant, Master Michael Vallier."

Then Sister Helena arrived and plunged into a

sensible practical conversation about the proper road to Mallowdale. "Can we get there by nightfall?" she demanded.

Arlette made a face behind the nun's back. Not by the quiver of a muscle did the boy reveal that he had seen it. But he answered with anxious gravity: "It would be wiser to come down with me to Hardraw. I know it would give my mother great pleasure to lodge you for the night."

2

Guests at Hardraw

IT WAS, OF COURSE—as Sister Helena did not fail to remark—only a very small castle, really no more than a tower. It had been built in the days of William Rufus. A flight of steps led up to the hall. The real ground floor was like a dark, cool cellar, shut in by ten-foot walls, windowless, and reached only by a staircase from above. It was used for stores, and there was a well cut down through the rock to a bubbling spring.

Michael's mother, Lady Isabella, came down the front steps as the strangers dismounted in the yard. Robert and Margery, round-eyed with interest, struggled hard to remember their manners. Visitors were almost unknown at Hardraw, and, truth to tell, their mother was nearly as excited as they were. She greeted Sister Helena with smiling dignity, joked with Arlette for a moment, and then took them up into the hall.

"Supper is nearly ready," she remarked. Arlette wrinkled up her nose appreciatively as she caught the savory smells drifting from the kitchen just inside. They had fared poorly for dinner, coming across the wastelands of the forest, and the hill air had made her ravenous.

Lady Isabella led them past the trestle table laid for the servants to the dais at the far end, where a maid was hastily adding two places to those set for the family.

"We do not stand on ceremony at Hardraw," she explained. "I am a widow—there are no gentlemen in the household—"

"Isn't Michael a gentleman?" demanded Margery.

"Not a very old one, my dear! Barely fifteen. He is still by rights a page. He should not sit down with the company—and still less should you children!—but I should get very tired of eating all my meals in solitary state. So if our guests will excuse the breach of etiquette—"

"I am fond of children," said Sister Helena magnificently.

"Robert," said his mother, "run to the kitchen and tell Sib to hurry with warm water. Our guests will want to wash. Michael, see that the two men are looked after, and have the baggage brought in."

She swept the two visitors up the private stair. It irked her a little that Hardraw had none of the privacy that gentlefolk were beginning to expect. It had been built with only one big room over the hall, in which all the family lived and slept. There was no other accommodation whatever, except for two curtained alcoves containing chests of clothes and such, and, of course, the two privy chambers recessed into the thickness of the outside wall and opening off the stairs. A brief acquaintance with the nun had already convinced Lady Isabella that it would be advisable to clear one of the alcoves and lay the visitors' bedding within.

"Your elder son—Michael?—he is old to be still at home?" said the nun, as she dried her face and hands.

"Yes. I—I scarcely know what is to happen about Michael."

"Indeed? I should have thought he could have been placed as a page in some nobleman's household."

"He *was* nearly two years with the late Lord Fleckney—"

"Ah," said Sister Helena quickly, "that unfortunate young man who was killed in the tournament not long ago?"

Lady Isabella nodded. "My own husband, Sir Robert, died in the same month."

"God rest his soul!"

"Once Michael was home, I fear I did not make all the effort I should have made to send him away again."

"It must be difficult," agreed Sister Helena diplomatically. She had already summed up the household as a very modest affair. So the husband had been a mere knight . . . Vallier? Vallier? It was not to be expected that she would recall the name. No wonder it had proved impossible to get the boy into another noble family! He was good-looking enough—but with only a knight for a father, and dead at that, he could hardly look for a great future.

Margery was shyly questioning Arlette as she tidied her hair. "And why is she taking you to Nottingham?"

"The king's there. I was sent for."

Margery's blue eyes widened. "Are you going to see him—to speak to him?" she said breathlessly.

"Yes. He's my guardian. You see, my father died when I was small—almost as young as your baby sister."

"My father's dead, too. But the king isn't *my* guardian."

"No?" Arlette smiled. "I expect it's because you have a mother still to look after you." She could hardly say that Margery did not look like an heiress. Only orphans like herself, with lands to inherit, became wards of the king.

"My father used to see the king nearly every day," said Margery. "Before he married Mother, that was."

"Sir Robert was one of the royal household," explained Lady Isabella, overhearing. "The king was always extremely kind to him."

"He used to send presents every Christmas!" Margery announced with pride.

"Did he, now?" said Sister Helena, permitting herself to smile. "They may say what they like against the king, but that is one thing I have *always* understood—he is most generous, and he never forgets his old servants."

"He's never sent me a Christmas present," Arlette grumbled comically.

"He has a great many wards—he has never seen most of them—and you of all people have no need of presents."

"If you are ready," said Lady Isabella, "I think we had better go down to supper."

They sat along one side of the high table, looking

down over the servants. Here was no great muster of valets and grooms, falconers and huntsmen, cooks and maids and washerwomen. At Hardraw there were only William the watchman, Hugh the porter, two other men for general duties, and three maids. By day, they shared the trestle table and the comfort of the fire. By night, they withdrew to the sides of the hall and slept, the men on the right and the maids on the left.

Lady Isabella sat at the middle of the high table with her guests on either side. Michael carved and served them, and filled their cups, as he had learned to do at Lord Fleckney's, before he took the stool by Arlette.

There had been no time to prepare a banquet for the unexpected arrivals, but it was a better supper than the Valliers had treated themselves to for many a long day. There was venison, and rabbits in gravy, pork and headcheese and chicken, followed by almonds, dates, and gingerbread. Old William, whose duties included keeping a sharp eye on the stores downstairs, had brought up some of the Gascony wine and some of the Anjou, as well as the customary homebrewed beer. It was a good meal, and they took their time.

"I must say," said Arlette, her dark eyes dancing, "it is a pleasant change to have someone to talk to at table."

"I suppose you weren't allowed to talk at the convent?"

"Not usually." Arlette's laugh was almost a gurgle. "We had to make signs. Like this!" She took her nose in her right hand and rubbed it up and down. "That

means, 'Pass the mustard.' And guess what this is."
She put her hands together and began to waggle
them over her plate.

Michael knitted his brows. "Is it a fish swimming?"

"Yes."

"Do some more," begged Robert shrilly.

"Well, there's a complete list of one hundred and
six signs," said Arlette good-humoredly. "I'll do a
few." She proceeded to do so, and was just convulsing
the children with a piece of dumb show which meant
that she wanted the milk when Sister Helena awoke
to what was happening, and sternly put an end to the
performance.

When all had finished, Lady Isabella rose to her
feet and the others followed suit. Before moving upstairs, Sister Helena beckoned to her two menservants and gave them orders for the morrow. Robert
and Margery flung themselves on Arlette, took a
hand each, and rushed her laughing through the
doorway. Michael had his first chance of private conversation with his mother.

"I suppose they *must* go in the morning?"

"Yes, dear. Sister has to see Arlette safely to court,
and then get back to her convent."

"Will Arlette stay at court?"

"Well, I expect the king will select a place for her
to live—until she marries. That shouldn't be long.
She's fourteen."

"No," agreed Michael thoughtfully. "Would you say
she was good-looking, Mother?"

"Oh, decidedly. Though of course black hair isn't
so fashionable as gold. And some might criticize her
nose—"

"It seems all right to me!" he interrupted.

"Well, there's no need to bite *mine* off, dear. In any case, even if she had the face of a horse, I should still prophesy early wedding bells for her. She is heiress to all the De la Garde lands—as the worthy sister has several times indicated to me since they arrived!"

There was just the faintest tartness in his mother's tone. She herself came of noble family, and Sir Robert, though a poor knight, had not been without aristocratic relations. She made up her mind to work these into the conversation if Sister Helena became any more irritating.

They were interrupted by the nun, who had just dismissed the menservants and mounted the dais again.

"It seems, madam, that we must trouble you a little further after all. Two of the horses have gone lame —which is scarcely surprising, when you think of the country those dolts dragged us over, by losing their way! John thinks that with a day's rest—if it would not be imposing too much on your hospitality—"

"Stay as long as you can, Sister—we shall be only too delighted," Lady Isabella assured her.

A pleasanter evening followed than Lady Isabella, at least, had expected. There was no doubt that all the children had taken to each other and Sister Helena—once you got used to her and made allowances —was a most stimulating guest. The two ladies found one common interest in fine needlework, at which Sister Helena was an expert, and another in the comparison of family trees. Every time Michael turned his head toward them they seemed to be thoroughly enjoying themselves.

". . . she was a Mortimer, one of the younger branch . . ."

". . . by her second marriage, to De Clare . . ."

"Would that be the De Clare who . . ."

"So that meant quartering his arms with . . ."

"Poor girl, widowed for the second time at nineteen . . ."

Michael wondered how women could go on like that, hour after hour, chattering of nothing but births, marriages, and deaths. Arlette's stories about the convent were much more amusing.

Suddenly, however, he became aware that something had happened. In their hunt through a forest of family trees, his mother and Sister Helena found something of real importance. They were facing each other openmouthed, and for the first time since supper there was a moment of silence between them. Then they burst out together:

"But if that is so . . ."

Both ladies stopped politely. His mother said: "I beg your pardon. You were going to say?"

"That if your late mother-in-law was a Grevel— and if the barony can be inherited through the female side—this should be of great interest to you for your son's sake!"

Michael knew it was ill-mannered to listen, but it was hard not to, after that last remark. He was relieved when his mother caught his eye and beckoned him over.

"Sister Helena has just given me a most interesting

piece of news," she said. "Lord Grevel—you have never seen him, but he was a distant cousin of your father's—died in an accident some months ago, a bridge swept away by floods. . . . His two children were drowned with him."

"God rest their souls!" said Michael automatically.

"But the point is—if his sister Beatrice died childless, as I seem to remember she did, and bearing in mind that your Uncle John was killed in the Crusade —you have a very good claim to the barony!"

"The barony? *Me?*"

"Through your grandmother," explained Sister Helena, her eyes alight with interest. "I have always understood that the Grevel barony was unusual—it is one of the few which can descend through the female line when no male heir exists. Of course, the lawyers would have to look into the terms of the original grant. If there is a rival branch of the family —or several rival branches," she added with gusto, "it should make a fascinating case."

"And an expensive one," said Lady Isabella, "which might drag on for years. I wonder what we ought to do."

"Do, madam?" Sister Helena sat up very straight. "There is only one possible thing to do. The boy must go to court at once, and make his claim!"

"Could he travel with us?" asked Arlette casually. "In this wild country the bigger the party, the better."

3

To the Court of the King

"YOU KNOW," said Michael slowly, his brown eyes troubled, "I am not sure after all that I want to go."

"Not sure?" Arlette flashed one of her keen bird's glances at him. "Oh," she burst out impulsively, "I can't understand you!"

It was the next morning, and now—to Michael at least—things did not seem as simple as they had seemed the previous night. In the castle all was happy, confident bustle. His mother was going through his clothes. In the kitchen they were baking some of his favorite pasties for the journey, and in the stables there was much polishing of harness and grooming of his mare, Sorelle. Everything was arranged. Michael was to ride with the others to Nottingham the next day, taking one of the Hardraw men, Dick o' the Dale, as his servant.

"What would you like to do?" Michael had asked Arlette after dinner.

"What *is* there to do?"

He had been a little taken aback. "We could go

27

hawking . . . or can you use a crossbow? Some girls can."

"I am not very good," she had admitted.

"Perhaps we had better not go far away, in case I am needed. And you won't want to do anything very tiring, I expect. Of course, we could play chess or checkers . . . or perhaps ninepins, or something with a ball—only then the young ones will insist on butting in—"

"Need we play anything? I had enough of games at the convent! Couldn't we just talk?"

So they went and sat on a huge gray rock overlooking a waterfall, and just talked. It was more of a change for Arlette. Boys interested her. They were like an unknown country that she had often seen at a distance but had never had a real chance to explore.

It was a clear and sunny day. The rock was warm under them, the flurry of the waterfall leaped and shone like pear blossom, and high across the river rose Walden Scar, pale golden, with the bracken above, stretching to the jagged skyline of Raven's Edge.

"What is it?" went on the girl. "Surely you don't mind leaving home for a while?"

"Of course not. If Lord Fleckney had not died, I should still be with him, anyhow. But this claim to the Grevel barony . . . I—I don't know."

"It's a wonderful chance. Haven't you *any* ambition?"

Michael waited for a few moments before answering. He was not used to serious conversation with the opposite sex. At Lord Fleckney's all the ladies had seemed artificial. They teased and bantered the whole time when they were not sulking or showing their cat's claws in malicious gossip. They were always acting if men were present.

Arlette was different; she was straightforward and candid. He could really talk to her, as though she were another boy.

"Yes," he admitted. "I *have* ambition, I suppose. But I want to get on by my own efforts—not because some particular kind of blood flows in my veins."

"But, Michael, isn't blood—family descent—the thing that matters? It's what makes the king the king. It's what makes us all what we are. You didn't breed your lovely deerhound from mongrels!"

"No. But I shall be just the same man, whether I'm recognized as Lord Grevel or stay plain Michael Vallier. I'm not changed just because those poor people were drowned when the bridge collapsed. It's all so—so accidental, so roundabout. Perhaps if my father had been Lord Grevel, I should have felt quite different. But I don't know. All souls are equal in the sight of God—I heard a friar say that in a sermon."

"That doesn't make them equal in the sight of man," said Arlette impatiently.

She had been brought up with the strongest sense of rank. She was not at all sure, even, that Michael's friar had been right. Heaven and Earth, she had been taught, were organized on very similar lines. Under God and the Virgin—as under King Henry and Queen Eleanor—there were the great barons of Heaven, the archangels, and below them the lesser barons, the ordinary angels. Somewhere in the

29

scheme came cherubim and seraphim, prophets and saints and martyrs, very much as the knights of the shires filled in the lower ranks of the gentry.

"No," Michael agreed. "Some people have to rule the others. I'd sooner be one of the rulers. But I'd sooner *make* myself one of them, by what I can do."

"You can't change your birth."

"It's hard. But it has been done. I mean, Father was only a knight's son, as I am. But he was one of the king's right-hand men. If he'd chosen to stay at court, he might have risen to—well, anything, almost."

"And you'd sooner do that?"

"I'll probably have to. Mother seems to think this claim is going to be easy. I have my doubts. If I ever rise in the world, I think it will be the hard, long way."

"There is of course a third route," Arlette said lightly.

"What is that?"

It was she who laughed this time, as she jumped up and smoothed her long crimson gown. "I'll tell you someday. We had better go back now."

They were off at sunrise, Michael in his best blue hood lined with silvery fur, a mulberry-colored tunic, and blue hose. Arlette wore a long gray gown, its quietness relieved by gold and silver threads woven into the fabric. She kept her dark head bare except for a plain velvet headband.

"I'm not wearing that stiff linen wimple in weather like this," she announced. "Time enough to be lady-like when I get to Nottingham."

Time enough for a great many things, she thought

to herself as they rode down the dale. Boys were lucky, she reflected, with a sidelong glance at Michael. They could make their own future, within limits. Even if that letter in Michael's wallet did not win him the Grevel barony—a letter to the king, laboriously composed last night by his mother, with much help from Sister Helena—at least it would rest mainly with Michael himself where he was ten years from now and what he was doing then. He would be either Lord Grevel or whatever his own efforts in the king's service had made him.

It was different for girls.

Arlette loved the old romances. Her fancy had fed on the tales of King Arthur and his knights, of Aucassin's love for Nicolette, of Tristram's for Isolde, but she knew that in real life things went differently. As heiress to a great estate, she would have plenty of men wishing to marry her. But she would have little choice. She must marry when and whom she was told. She prayed night and morning that it would be someone bearable, someone more or less her own age. But if it suited the king, it could just as easily be a widower of fifty, with a family older than herself, or a baby still squalling in his cradle. Noble marriages were not made for love, but to seal alliances and join estates.

These forebodings were driven out of her mind as they rounded a spur and a fresh view unfolded before her eyes. She enjoyed riding and could never be miserable for long when she felt the rhythm of a horse under her and saw the next bend in the road beckoning her forward.

So, hour by hour, then day by day, they rode south

4

Heart of Wax

"AND THIS LETTER to the Sheriff of Norfolk," said the man by the window, without turning around.

"Yes, my liege?" The clerk's quill paused in its scratching.

"Tell him, 'as he loves the king and his honor and his own safety, to seek out thirty barrels of the best and most exquisite herrings.' And say, 'for the king's own eating.'"

"Yes, my liege."

"Is the letter written to the Constable of the Tower of London? Let me see it. . . . Those alterations must be done before I stay there again, though it cost a hundred pounds. The smell of the drains made my rooms unbearable! Write in, 'as he values his life and liberty.'"

"I will, my liege."

"That is all. Have the letters sealed and sent off. One must be firm with these people."

There was no great firmness, however, in the face which smiled and nodded dismissal as the clerk gathered up parchment and inkhorn, and left the royal chamber.

At fifty-five Henry of Winchester was a good-looking, stoutish man of medium height, with a weakness about the mouth that his beard did not altogether hide. If there was self-will in that face there was also kindliness—and a certain amount of self-will might surely be expected in one who had been king almost ever since he could remember. It was now nearly half a century since that day in Gloucester Abbey when, as a small boy still bewildered by the sudden death of his father, he had heard himself proclaimed Henry the Third, King of England, Lord of Ireland, Duke of Aquitaine. All his life since then, his rank had set him apart from other men.

A page lifted the curtain and bowed from the doorway.

"If it please you, my liege—"

"Well, Thomas, who is it?"

"The Lady Arlette de la Garde, answering your royal summons. With her is a young gentleman, Michael Vallier, son of the late Sir Robert Vallier—"

"Poor Robert! How time passes! Bring them in."

Again the curtain lifted. Arlette came in, holding herself very straight in her best blue gown, her dark hair carefully dressed under the stiff white linen wimple. After her, duskily magnificent, sailed Sister Helena. Michael brought up the rear, dropping on one knee as the ladies curtsied.

The king came to them with outstretched hands.

"So you are Arlette! You have blossomed. Have you been properly looked after since you arrived?"

"The chamberlain has been most kind, my liege," broke in Sister Helena. "Our quarters are most comfortable."

35

The king turned to Michael. "And you are Sir Robert's eldest son? You have his eyes."

"You have a good memory, my liege," Michael blurted out, surprised. It was quite true. Everyone said he had the same brown eyes as his father, bright as a moorland stream dancing down through the peat.

"Sir Robert served me well. I don't forget such men. I was sorry when he asked for Hardraw and retired from court. But no doubt it was a happier place to rear a family." He smiled again. "There is nothing better than a happy family, my boy—I thank Heaven daily for mine. But what brings you here? You were not summoned."

"I have a letter, my liege. From my mother."

The king took it curiously and broke the seal. Watching, Michael noticed how his left eyelid drooped, giving him a shrewd, almost crafty expression when seen from that side. But, as he learned later, it was purely physical. His eldest son, the Lord Edward, though utterly different in character, had inherited the same odd feature.

"H'm . . . the Grevel barony . . . a big matter, my boy. You understand that?"

"Yes, my liege."

"This must be investigated. I will hand it over to my officers. Nothing would please me more than to see Sir Robert's son enrolled among my lords. But you will realize, a barony is not just a favor that even the king can hand out at will."

"I am not asking for favors, my liege. Only for what is right," said Michael respectfully. "It is not my own wish to come. I have to, for the sake of my

younger brothers and sisters. They have the next
claim after me. And—and—" he concluded awkwardly, "there may be others later to consider, when
I am a man and marry."

"Quite right, my boy. Well, we shall see. Thomas!"
The page bobbed through the doorway. "Conduct the
Lady Arlette to the queen's chamber—say I shall be
there directly. As you go, hand in this letter at the
Chancery and tell them to look into it. Put Master
Vallier in the charge of Hugo Best—he was a friend
of Sir Robert's in the old days; he will be glad to see
his son."

The boys bowed, the ladies curtsied, and the in-
terview was over.

That was the last Michael heard of his claim for some
days and almost the last he saw of Arlette, safely in-
stalled among the queen's ladies. Such a multitude
thronged the fortress and overflowed into the town
below that the young friends caught only an occa-
sional glimpse of each other.

Michael spent much of his time with his father's
old colleague, Hugo Best, a lean, hook-nosed clerk
with humorous eyebrows arched over twinkling blue
eyes. He was a rare character, a man of peasant
blood who had raised himself out of the furrows by
exceptional intelligence. His village parson had noticed him as a child and given him schooling above
his class. Later he had taken holy orders of the low-
est kind, without ever going on to become a full
priest.

"Why?" Hugo echoed, when Michael asked. "Use
your brain, boy. How else can a poor man enter the

king's service—how else can he learn to read and write? Isn't every office staffed with clerks in holy orders? Yet how many are ordained full priests? Once they are, it's good-bye to any thought of marrying, and that," he laughed, "is a sacrifice not every man is willing to make, even in the king's service."

Hugo, of course, was unique. He had everything at his fingertips. People said that only Heaven and Hugo Best understood the workings of the king's government—and judging by the results it must be Hugo who played the more active part. He had taken a fancy to Michael, and, finding him interested, he taught him all he could.

"I owe it to you," he said dryly. "Your father did me a good turn once."

"What was that?"

The clerk chuckled. "He got out of my way. Leaving the court when he did. He was the worst rival I had—good friends though we were. You see, the odds were on his side. He had the blood as well as the brains."

"You're not afraid of *me* as a rival?" Michael asked mischievously.

"You're still a boy. When you're old enough to be dangerous, I shall have got where I want to be."

So, sitting at Hugo's elbow in a chamber of Nottingham Castle, Michael began to probe into the mystery that had often fascinated him—how England was really governed, what the link was between the plowman trudging behind his oxen and the monarch on his throne, and how one man could make sure that his word, spoken in Westminster, would be obeyed in Cornwall and Northumberland.

In theory, Hugo explained, the king ruled with the help of the Great Council of barons, together with the bishops and the most powerful abbots.

"But they can't be making the journey every month —they have their own estates to manage—so the king calls them only now and again, when there's something of special importance. The real control, you might say, under the king of course, is in the hands of four men. There's the justiciar, who is the king's deputy and can issue writs under his seal; there's the chancellor, who runs the Chancery—the secretarial side of the government, that is, as you can guess from all these letters and records; and of course there's the treasurer."

"You said four."

"So I did. The fourth's the chief forester. Except where the royal forests are affected, he doesn't bother us much."

Under these four principal ministers, Michael learned, came many important officers—the barons of the Exchequer, the royal justices, the sheriffs, the constables of the various castles dotted up and down the country, and the leading members of the king's household, who accompanied him on all his travels.

"Why *does* he travel so much?" Michael asked. "I suppose it's so that he can see things for himself?"

Hugo covered a smile with his hand. "Of course, of course. He is most conscientious. . . . There is also, however, the problem of feeding this multitude—not to mention its hundreds of horses. The court descends on each place in turn like a plague of locusts, empties the countryside of food and fodder, and then packs up and rides on again. As we shall have to do

39

from Nottingham in a week or two, if we are not to go hungry."

Michael could see the force of that argument. Nottingham had only about fifteen hundred inhabitants, and the arrival of the court meant a huge increase in the number of mouths to be fed. Apart from the officials of the household and the government, there was a staff of clerks, an escort of two dozen archers, a dozen messengers ready day and night to mount and carry dispatches anywhere, and a host of squires, pages, valets, grooms, falconers, huntsmen, kennelmen, cooks, carters, and packhorse men. And there were all those who flocked uninvited to the king wherever he was—people like himself, with genuine business, and every kind of hanger-on.

The king, Hugo explained, had four sources of income that could be roughly estimated in advance. There was the revenue from his own lands. There was the output of the mines, especially the west country tin. There was income from the royal forests, and the profits on coining and exchanging money.

"The rest is more uncertain," said Hugo, ticking off the items on his fingers. "There's taxes and customs duties; various fines and penalties; monopolies and special favors—now and again he has to squeeze the foreign moneylenders; and of course heirs and heiresses, who're wards of the Crown."

"Heirs and . . . heiresses?"

"Oh, yes. When it comes to arranging their marriages. If the other family wants the match badly enough, they'll offer him good money to agree. It's an investment from their point of view—and for the king it's an extremely useful source of extra income."

"What is the king really like?" asked Michael suddenly. "I mean, he is kind, isn't he? I know they say he is very extravagant, that he's always wanting money for luxuries, but he wouldn't make a girl marry someone she hated—especially when he's promised not to?"

"Oh, he's promised, has he?" said Hugo slowly. They had paused beside the spigurnel—the officer responsible for sealing the day's letters. For a few moments Hugo did not speak again. With a smile he watched the first blob of molten red fall and flatten on the parchment, and then, at the quick pressure of the seal, cool and harden into a tiny picture.

"We have several seals," said Hugo, "the wax takes the impression of whichever one is applied."

"Of course—"

"Do you know what the king is sometimes called by those who know him best? Heart of wax!"

5

Enter the Earl

ARLETTE, MEANWHILE, was vastly enjoying her first taste of court life.

After the first shy day or two, she took her place happily among the queen's ladies. Queen Eleanor herself was gracious to her—affectionate in her impulsive French way—and Arlette thought her fascinating. No wonder that still, after nearly thirty years of married life, the king was devoted to her! Her father had been Raymond Berenger, Count of Provence, and himself one of the poets who had made that region famous as the land of troubadours. She was one of four lovely sisters who had all married kings, like in a fairy tale. Margaret had married Louis IX of France and Beatrice his younger brother Charles, later King of Sicily. Sanchia had married King Henry's brother Richard, the Earl of Cornwall, who, though he was no real king, was called King of the Romans. Four sisters, two pairs of brothers— what could have been more romantic?

It was Eleanor who had brought new fashions into England, such as the long, trailing gown with scalloped edges, which you had to lift gracefully with one hand when you walked. And it was Eleanor, the poet's daughter, who had encouraged the king in his love of elegance.

"When I do marry," Arlette promised herself, "at least I will have a wonderful home." She resolved to have everything, as far as possible, as the king and queen would have had it. She would sleep between silken sheets on a mattress covered with velvet, and the bed would be spread with cloth of gold from Genoa. She would drink from a glass cup set in crystal, and her lord from a handsome coconut shell mounted on silver. Smoky fireplaces would be replaced with chimneys and carved overmantels in the French style. How cozy to sit by the fire on a cold day and study the little pictures!

There would be bigger pictures to hide the bare walls, not only in tapestry but in painted cloth, which the king preferred, because it gave a smoother effect. When Arlette admired the decoration of the queen's chamber at Nottingham—a series showing the adventures of Alexander the Great—she was told about the other royal lodgings. She must see the paintings of the history of Antioch at the Tower of London, and the siege of Acre by Richard Coeur de Lion at Clarendon. Not all the subjects were so grand. The king had a personal taste for rather pretty schemes—pale-green backgrounds powdered with golden stars or dotted with birds and animals. Arlette rather agreed.

She might even—to be thoroughly up to date— have a bath fitted, so that the dirty water could run straight out through a hole in the wall, down into the moat. It would be worth asking Sister Helena to stay, merely to see her face! Though the convent rules

43

provided for five baths per year, Sister Helena had always felt that there was something rather sinful about removing all one's clothes and enjoying, actually *enjoying*, a wallow in hot water.

It was the younger Eleanor—Eleanor of Castile, the lovely young Spanish wife of the king's elder son —who had startled English society with this new-fangled notion of fitted baths. Arlette was longing to see her and her husband, who sounded like some dashing hero of romance. But the Lord Edward was fighting the Welsh rebels, and Eleanor was awaiting the birth of their first child.

How different this family was, thought Arlette, from some of the royal families in past times, when son had rebelled against father, and brother against brother. But then the king was so kind, not only to his own family but to everybody; the court was full of his wife's relatives for whom he had found positions in England. He never forgot anyone, however humble, who had served him well, and would always show his gratitude whether by sending a fur-lined cloak to the wife of the royal fiddler, or by a yearly payment to the old woman who had nursed him as a child.

How could such a king have enemies? thought Arlette in her simplicity. Then Simon de Montfort, Eart of Leicester, came back to court from abroad.

"And now," Hugo Best told Michael, "we may look for trouble again."

Michael had no need to ask why. The bad feeling between the king and the earl was common gossip.

Several years ago, in 1258, the Great Council had met at Oxford and put a number of demands before

44

the king. If he wanted money, he must let the real government of the country pass into the hands of a small number of powerful barons. Simon de Montfort was not the originator of these demands but he had come, more and more, to be the leader of the movement.

The king had agreed at first. Then the pope had released him from his promise, because it had been given under threat of force. Simon had gone abroad for nearly two years, and the king had used the time to regain his power, putting back the officials he had been made to dismiss and appointing loyal commanders to the key fortresses throughout the country.

"Afraid of Simon?" murmured Hugo. "Of course he is! He has said so himself."

There were two opinions about Simon, just as there were about the king. It was the first matter on which Michael and Arlette seriously disagreed.

They had met, in the cool of the evening, on the battlements crowning the sandstone precipice. Below, the small River Leen wound lazily through the marshes to join the Trent. The clack of watermills came up through the still air. The small green hills, Wilford and Colwick and the others, slept in the last sunshine, and farther south, blue and misty, hung the dim distances of Charnwood.

It was not easy to get a word together. Michael's position was still doubtful, and he could not move easily among the queen's ladies. However, Arlette had the will and found the way.

"I hate that man," she whispered as the earl stalked by.

Michael looked after him curiously. Like everyone

else, he was rather frightened of that stalwart figure with the hard-bitten features and the prominent eyes. Though nearly sixty, De Montfort still carried himself like a Crusader. Everyone admitted he was the foremost soldier of this time, and Michael found it impossible not to admire him.

"Penniless adventurer!" said Arlette viciously.

"But he's the king's brother-in-law—"

"I know! He came over to England with nothing. He tricked the king into letting him marry his sister—and they say it isn't a proper marriage at all—"

"Why ever not?"

"She was a widow, and she'd taken a solemn vow never to marry again. He got around her somehow."

"He's supposed to be a very religious man."

"Oh, yes! To hear some people talk, you'd think he were a saint, almost!" She tossed her dark head irritably. "He does a great deal of praying, night and morning, but deeds count more than words. What about his oath of allegiance to the king? Why doesn't he keep it?"

"Well, some people do say that the king is . . . changeable."

"The king is charming! A dear!"

"Yes, I know. But—" Michael stopped, warned by her expression. He changed his tack. "There is something in what they say about the court being too full of foreigners."

"I like that! When the earl is a complete foreigner himself! De Montfort champion of the English! I find that extremely amusing."

It was useless to go on wrangling. It was better to change the subject.

"Is anything settled about the claim yet?" she asked.

"No, it may drag on for months. There's another claimant, some remote cousin, on his way home from Greece. It all turns on one word in the original grant."

"One word?"

"Yes. Usually the wording goes, 'and to his heirs male for ever.' But the word 'male' is left out in the Grevel barony, so our side will say it means either sex."

"Obviously."

"Hugo says nothing is obvious to lawyers, especially when there's so much at stake. The other side will argue that it was just a slip of the clerk's pen, and that 'heir' means a male unless it definitely says otherwise. In that case I can't possibly inherit through my grandmother, and this Lord Sleddale will get the barony."

"Why should he want to be a lord twice over?"

"The Grevel estates aren't entirely without value," said Michael in a dry tone he had caught from Hugo. "A castle on the Wye, a house in London—"

"Nearly as big as my own estate! I think it's *most* unfair. I shall ask the queen about it."

"For Heaven's sake, don't!" he begged. "Things aren't done like that."

"All right. But it would be much more sensible if they were."

The days passed pleasantly. There were rides over the leafy ridges of Sherwood or to the airy crags overlooking Charnwood, hawking parties, and walks in

the river meadows. The evenings were given up to
singing and dancing and storytelling, to noisy games
like blindman's buff and quiet ones like chess, or just
to conversation and strolling in the rose garden.

After the first two weeks Arlette decided that she
would have enjoyed it all even more if she could
have had some idea of what was planned for her. Presumably the king would not have summoned her
without having some intention. Perhaps—it was not
altogether a pleasant thought—she was being quietly
looked over as somebody's possible bride. It was not
a matter on which a young maiden could ask blunt
questions, but the suspense grew, day by day, until
she was driven to fish for information by means of
casual remarks to carefully chosen individuals.

The result was not encouraging.

"But, my dear," said Yolande de Clifford. "I thought
everybody knew. Isn't it all arranged?"

"What?" Arlette contained herself with difficulty.

"The Weardale boy—Peter—"

"What's he like?"

"I met him at Windsor last Christmas—we called
him monkey face."

"How old?" asked Arlette dismally.

"Ten, I should think. By now." Yolande laughed. "So
there's no *hurry*. Though of course the king may
want you to go through a ceremony very soon."

It was not quite as definite as Yolande pretended,
in her bubbling know-all way, but some of the other
girls confirmed that there had been plenty of talk
about the match. The Weardales were keen to join the
De la Garde estates with their own. The king liked

them and favored the idea: it was going to be made well worth his while. It was also true that the child Peter, besides being heir to his father's lands, had inherited his father's puny build and somewhat sub-human features.

Arlette rushed away to the chapel and prayed hard for deliverance. Within twenty-four hours it seemed that her prayers had been answered, though not at all in the way she would have chosen.

Thomas the page summoned her to the king's presence. Earl Simon was there. From their faces she could see that there had been a quarrel, and who had won.

"You had better tell her yourself," said the king crossly.

Simon nodded and turned a severe eye upon her. "We have been discussing your future, young lady. It is time we thought of a husband for you."

"I am in no hurry, my lord. I—I am so young—"

"Plenty of girls of your age get married. But no matter. As things stand, there is sure to be some delay."

Arlette summoned up all her courage. Her whole life's happiness might be at stake. "My Lord, I do not want to marry some boy even younger than myself—"

She stopped. Simon stared down at her. "There is no suggestion that you should." He turned and looked meaningly at the king. "Is there, my liege?"

"No . . . oh, no . . . not now."

Arlette moistened her lips. "Then may I ask—*who* —my lord?"

"Certainly. The Earl of Renfield."

"But—" She gasped, looking from the one to the other unbelievingly. "The Earl of Renfield is married —the countess was here with him only last week—"

"That is why there will be some delay," said Simon gravely. "The earl has discovered a fault in this marriage. It appears that he and the countess are related— distantly, but within the limits forbidden by the Church. It is, therefore, no marriage. Such cases are not uncommon."

"Only when a man wishes to get rid of his wife!" she burst out furiously.

"Silence!" And she stopped, because he had a voice like thunder. "It is no business of yours to know better than the Church," he went on more quietly. "As I say, nothing can be done in a hurry. The case will go to Rome. It will be months, perhaps a year, before the Earl of Renfield is free. Meanwhile, it is the king's wish that you should live with some noble family until your marriage."

Arlette turned pointedly to the king. "I obey *your* wishes, my liege. But the Earl of Leicester has no right to meddle with my affairs."

The king looked uncomfortable. "No one is meddling. We are thinking only of your happiness."

"I quite understand that I must live somewhere—"

"That is why I am sending you to my own sister at Kenilworth."

Arlette's angry flush faded to the pallor of misery. "Your sister, my liege? You mean—Earl Simon's wife?"

"We shall be happy to have you," said Simon.

Again she studied their faces. She could see that any protest would be wasted. She said, chokingly, "Have I

50

leave to retire?" Before the king could even speak, Simon answered for him. "Certainly. Everything is settled."

She ducked under the curtain in the doorway and almost ran down the echoing corridor, just managing to get out of earshot before the sobs of helpless fury broke forth.

6

Civil War?

Two DAYS LATER, after much packing up and general bustle, the court moved south.

The queen and one or two other ladies traveled in cumbersome four-wheel carriages, drawn by several horses in single file. The carriages were arched overhead, painted and gilded at great cost, strewn with embroidered cushions, and hung with tapestries and silken curtains at the windows. They were very magnificent.

"But, oh, so bumpy!" Arlette confided to Michael with deep feeling, after trying one for a couple of miles. "You feel every rut and stone—and all the cushions in the world don't seem much use." She had got over the first shock of the king's decision and was facing the immediate future with her usual determination to make the best of things.

When the court reached Leicester, Earl Simon's party turned off along the road to Kenilworth. Sadly Michael and Arlette said good-bye. It was to be a long time before—in very different circumstances—they would meet again.

"London is the most marvelous place in the world," Michael wrote to Arlette a few weeks later. He was a better hand with a pen than most boys. Gentlemen were inclined to look down on reading and writing as occupations fit only for clerks, but Michael thought it foolish to put oneself at the mercy of one's inferiors in such an important matter.

"You *must* write," Arlette had told him. "I am going to be lonely at Kenilworth. You have your family at Hardraw, but I have nobody."

So Michael wrote: "At present I am staying in the palace of Westminster, a mile or two out in the country, where the king likes to watch the work on the new abbey church. But sometimes I am sent with messages to the Tower, and I can either go down by river or ride the whole length of the city; or walk, if there is no hurry, and turn down any side street which looks interesting. You would not believe the number of people—so many strangers and even foreigners coming and going the whole time. I have found a public eating house among the wineshops down by the Thames. You can go there almost any hour of the day or night and find anything you fancy, freshly cooked and piping hot."

He told her about the sales of thoroughbred horses, held every Friday in a field outside the walls. Everybody, courtiers and citizens alike, went out to see them put through their paces. He felt envious of the apprentices playing football: he would love to join in, but of course it was not a proper sport for one of his class. However, there was soon to be a mock battle staged in these fields, and any boy of rank who had not yet been knighted could take part.

"If I break my neck," he added, "I will tell you in my next letter."

There was still no news of his claim to the barony. As there was no place for him as a page at court, the king had arranged for him to enter the household of the constable of the Tower, at least for the time being.

"I shall enjoy living in the heart of London, though I shall miss old Hugo Best, who of course has to travel around with the Chancery clerks wherever the king goes. Another thing is, I shall not be able to send letters direct by the royal messengers in future— which is a pity, because there is always somebody going between the king and Kenilworth. Still, if you will write to me in the care of Hugo Best, he says he can enclose it with the next batch of royal mail for the Tower. It will be rather a roundabout method sometimes, but it will be as quick as any other and much safer—nobody dares to touch a royal messenger."

He was about to seal the letter when it struck him that there was not a word about Arlette herself in it. That would not do. Girls were such self-centered creatures. He took up his quill again and scrawled: "I hope you are happy at Kenilworth. I expect there is good riding in the Forest of Arden. I hope the king's sister is kind to you, and that you like Earl Simon more than you thought you would. He is very popular in London, among the people. They all say what a fine man he is."

Much to his annoyance she never answered.

Before the summer was out, normal contact with Kenilworth became difficult. Things were going from bad to worse between the king and his brother-in-law.

First—without the king's knowledge—Simon had called the barons to a meeting at Oxford. They issued an ultimatum. The demands made at that earlier conference there, the famous Provisions of Oxford, must be accepted. Anyone opposing them must be proclaimed an outlaw.

This tone was more than even Henry could stand. He refused. Simon gathered an army, marched to the Welsh border, seized the Bishop of Hereford in his own cathedral, threw him into a dungeon, and confiscated his goods. The bishop, who came from Savoy, was the most hated of all the foreigners the king had brought into England. It was widely agreed that he had got no more than he deserved.

It was different when Simon wheeled across England, expelling the king's sheriffs and castellans from their places, and confiscating the property of all who opposed him. Worcester and Salisbury surrendered without a fight, Gloucester after a four-day siege. Simon swept on to Reading, avoided Windsor, which was held by the king's son, and struck down through Guildford and Reigate to the Channel ports. There he failed to capture Dover but was able to cut off all direct contact between the king and France.

In this month of crisis Michael found himself once more at court, for the king and queen had sought safety in the Tower. It was a rather precarious kind of safety. The citizens were solidly in favor of De Montfort, and the Tower was practically blockaded.

"Faults on both sides," commented Hugo, after a cautious glance around. "True, we have too many foreigners in high places. But the earl is the last person who should mention that."

"I suppose the king *is* extravagant?"

"All kings are extravagant." The clerk's blue eyes

twinkled. "If it is not one thing, it is another. With King Henry it's building, and with his uncle the Lion Heart it was fighting. Which is better, to build Westminster Abbey or to kill Saracens? The root of the trouble is something none of them realizes. Things cost more than they used to, and the king's income never grows as fast as his expenses. King Henry the Second could enlist mercenary knights at eightpence a day—his grandson would scarcely get them for three times as much. It's the same with everything. I don't say that good government isn't better than bad, or economy better than waste, but with things as they are it would take the wisdom of King Solomon himself to make ends meet."

"Then you don't think that it will make much difference, even if the earl gets his way?"

"Not so far as money is concerned. In other ways, perhaps it will. But it is not for me to express opinions." Hugo's face became a bland mask again. Only in his eyes the impish intelligence still danced with amusement. "I am only a clerk."

Hugo would never explain beyond a certain point. Facts, yes—the way things were done in Chancery and in the Exchequer. Opinions, no. Hugo was far too cautious.

"Make up your own mind," he would say, and turn again to his parchment rolls.

Michael could not make up his mind. He liked the king as a person, but he could see his weaknesses. He was not attracted by the grim Earl Simon, but he could not help admiring him as a great general and statesman. Was a man, however great, entitled to revolt against the anointed king, to whom he had sworn

allegiance? Again, though, was a king entitled to behave as Henry seemed to, sometimes?

For once Michael was glad that he was not grown
up, and not acknowledged as Lord Grevel, forced to
take sides. Once, on a spoiled scrap of parchment,
Hugo demonstrated to him what he called the "arithmetic of power."

There were over two hundred baronies in England,
controlling something like a hundred and forty castles. Their size was reckoned in "knights' fees," the
number of knights each baron was expected to pro-
vide in war. There were great baronies like the earldom of Gloucester, with its three castles and three
hundred knights' fees, the earldoms of Leicester itself, Arundel, Norfolk, and several others with well
over a hundred knights' fees—including the earldom
of Chester, with two hundred, held by the king's elder
son. Then there were the smaller fry, like Lord Sleddale, Michael's rival for the inheritance. There were
bishops ruling large domains and controlling
armed forces. Finally, there were baronies held by old
or sick men, who might manage to remain neutral
in a crisis, or by children, who could also avoid making any awkward decision.

So it was not just a question of how many barons
joined Simon, and how many remained loyal to the
king. It was important to know *which* barons—how
many castles they held and where, and their total
power in terms of the knights who would follow them
if it came to civil war.

"It is very rough-and-ready arithmetic," Hugo
warned him. "Barons change sides suddenly! Then
figures jump out of one column and into another,

which would be very upsetting if it happened in the treasurer's accounts."

Michael saw now why Simon had put a stop to the plan that Arlette should marry a Weardale, which would have shifted more than forty knights to the king's side. The Earl of Renfield, for whom she was now intended, was a hot supporter of his own. Might it not also explain the long dispute over the Grevel barony? Lord Sleddale was a small but useful ally of Simon, who would be a good deal more useful when his estates were joined with the thirty-seven knights' fees of Grevel. Michael himself was a little young to matter, yet; but Simon would tend to regard him as a king's man, like his father, and would not wish him to succeed in his claim.

The constable of the Tower was another who had no doubt of his new page's loyalty to the king. One morning he beckoned Michael.

"The queen is leaving at once. It is not very pleasant for her here, with the London rabble catcalling outside. She is going to join the Lord Edward at Windsor."

"Yes, sir?"

"I want you to accompany her in the royal barge. It is, of course, quite unsafe for her to leave by road."

7

A Quiet Life at Kenilworth

THEY WERE READY. The broad, flat-bottomed barge, gay with paint and gilding, canopied against the sun, lay alongside the Water Gate. The queen's baggage was stowed aboard. Now, with the king at her elbow murmuring reassurances, Eleanor of Provence came down to the river.

"You will be better off at Windsor, my dear."

"I hope so." She shivered. "These Londoners are like wolves howling at the gates."

They kissed. He handed her into the barge. He looked very pale. Poor man, thought Michael, he had never been a soldier and he was too old to start now. Royal dignity forbade that he too should run from the threats of his own unruly subjects—but how much happier he would have been to be going with his wife, away from London to the safety of Windsor and the support of his warrior son.

The ladies, the squires and pages, the small armed escort, were all aboard. The rowers pushed off. Soon they would be out of the danger zone of the city.

They steered for the middle of the river. The Tower

fell astern. London Bridge lay ahead, marching across the water on its twenty narrow arches, lined on both sides with shops and houses.

There was a fortified tower, commanding the thirteenth arch, built in the form of a drawbridge, to let tall-masted craft pass up and down.

As the barge drew nearer, Michael could see that this strip of the bridge was crowded with people. So, too, were the tower and the houses stretching to right and left. The windows were filled with faces. Apprentices had clambered to the topmost gables and crouched there perilously, dark figures against the scudding clouds.

A low murmur, menacing and heart-chilling, ran along the bridge as these watchers recognized the barge. Michael stole a glance at the queen. Her olive face was sallower than usual, but she sat upright, her anger conquering her fear. She had more fight in her than the king. Not a wise woman, perhaps, but a woman of spirit.

Her ladies were parchment pale. The archers fingered their crossbows uneasily. The oarsmen, with their backs to the danger, pulled stolidly in perfect rhythm. But Michael saw one lick his lips, and the beads of sweat break out upon another's forehead.

They were close enough now to make out actual words shouted from the bridge.

"Take her back!"

"Take her back to Provence while you're at it!"

There were jeers about foreigners in general and the queen's relatives in particular. Taunts about her extravagance, personal insults, actual threats. . . .

Now they were very near indeed. The houses rose like a cliff, blotting out the sky. Stones thudded on the canopy and rattled in the bottom of the barge. An archer swore under his breath, and one of the ladies screamed. Filthy water splashed down on the prow, and stinking rubbish showered from every window within range. Men and women leaned out, holding pots and pails. Michael noticed scufflings as the shopkeepers tried to interfere. They had no grudge against the queen, whose love of luxury had brought them profitable business. It was the mob that had seized the bridge and occupied the houses.

The barge lost way and came almost to a standstill as this hail of stones and filth descended upon the rowers. "Shall we shoot, madam?" asked the captain of the escort. He spoke without eagerness. His small number of archers, shooting upward at a difficult angle, could never clear the bridge of its defenders. The only result would be to infuriate them. Then, from being offensive, they would pass to being really dangerous. One heavy object, dropped into the barge as it went under the bridge, would tear a hole in the bottom and throw them all into the river.

The queen saw the situation as clearly as he did. The mob was determined that she should not pass, and to try would endanger the lives of all. "No," she said, "turn around. Take us back to the Tower."

Meanwhile life was less exciting for Arlette.

True, Kenilworth was one of the great castles of England, rising from its island in a man-made lake. But, though the Countess of Leicester shared many of her kingly brother's expensive tastes, she could not make the castle he had given her a very lighthearted establishment.

Countess Eleanor had now turned fifty. (How confusing they are, thought Arlette, all these Eleanors! Not content with having a sister and a cousin of this name, the king had married a third Eleanor and acquired yet a fourth as daughter-in-law.) The countess had lost her first husband, the Earl of Pembroke, while she was no more than a girl. Then she had married the stern French soldier, Simon. They had had seven children; five of them boys and now grown up, most of them hard fighters like their father. One was in holy orders—but that again was not so unlike his father, for Simon was religious enough in a joyless way. He knew the Church services as well as any priest, liked talking to learned bishops, and hated Jews and heretics.

Arlette saw little of Simon, or of his sons. They were more often riding up and down the country, raising troops or besieging castles. Only the ladies stayed at Kenilworth, embroidering till the mere sight of a needle roused Arlette to a fury of irritation.

What did the countess think of the crisis? she often wondered. It must be a strange, troubling situation, with husband and sons on one side and practically at war with brother and nephew on the other.

People said she had been a flirt in her younger days. She was different now. She had put her foot down about Michael's letter.

"Who is this Michael Vallier? What right has he to send you letters?"

"But there's nothing in the letter," Arlette protested. "We are only friends—"

"Friends! What would the Earl of Renfield say?"

"I am not in the least interested, madam," said Arlette, tilting her chin as defiantly as she dared.

"You should be! You are practically betrothed to him."

"I cannot be until Rome decides whether he is single or married already."

"A girl of your age must consider her good name."

"Don't you think, madam," retorted Arlette wickedly, "that just a tiny blot on my good name would make me a better match for the Earl of Renfield? If he gets rid of one wife because he fancies the estates of a second, *his* name will look as though it's been spattered with an inkhorn!"

"You will be ruled by me," said the countess, breathing hard. "You have been placed under my supervision. You will not correspond with this youth in London."

Nor was Arlette able to, though she did her best to smuggle a letter out of the castle by private messenger. The countess discovered and stopped it.

The uneasy summer waned. There was shocked chuckling among the Kenilworth ladies when they heard of the queen's adventure at London Bridge. It was said that her lanky son had gone into one of his towering rages when the story reached him at Windsor. Never would he forgive the Londoners for this insult to his mother! Arlette, sitting silent and apart from the other ladies, glowered in sympathy. She had never met the Lord Edward, but she knew and loved the queen. Also she knew, but did not love, the cats of Kenilworth, as she named them to herself in private. If only the king would stand up to his enemies, or even give his son a chance to do so!

But the next news was that the king had given way. Earl Simon was off to meet him in London. The Great Council was summoned to St Paul's. There was a great deal of talk there, and some squabbling among the king's opponents—Simon was much displeased with his chief ally, Gilbert de Clare, the Earl of Gloucester. "I don't trust that man," said the mistress of Kenilworth darkly. "I hope my lord will not place too much reliance upon him." To Arlette this incident came as a faint ray of hope, feeling as she did almost a prisoner in the De Montfort camp.

Autumn drifted on. The leaves of Arden came rustling earthward, the lake grew with the rains and spread like a sheet of pewter under the gray sky. King and earl crossed to Boulogne, to lay their dispute before King Louis of France as umpire. When they came back, the queen stayed behind in France.

"And I don't blame her," said Arlette, snapping off a thread with her teeth, "until some of her subjects learn to behave! And I do *not* refer to the London rabble."

So 1263 passed into 1264. In January the French king published his decision. First, the Provisions of Oxford—already denounced by two popes in succession—were null and void. Second, the barons should return all the castles they had seized. Third, King Henry should be free in future to choose all his own officers. Fourth, the foreigners driven out of England should be free to return.

It was a complete defeat for De Montfort.

"What do you expect?" sneered one of the Kenilworth ladies, "when Louis is King Henry's brother-in-law!"

"Not every man stands by his brother-in-law," Arlette retorted. "Some behave quite differently!"

"Oh, *you*," said the other lady with withering contempt. And later, when they were all playing with a ball, she nearly contrived to hit Arlette in the eye. Arlette was too quick for her, however, and ducked. For the rest of the game, whenever the ball was in Arlette's hand, her enemy looked miserably anxious. Arlette found it much more satisfactory to leave her permanently in suspense than to commit any definite act of revenge.

About that time, Earl Simon was thrown from his horse and fractured a bone in his leg, no light matter at his age. Even Arlette could not help but admire the determination with which he refused to lie up and be nursed at home but struggled around the country in a carriage, organizing his supporters for a second round of civil war.

As soon as the winter floods died down and the roads hardened enough for the passage of troops, the trouble began again, as though King Louis's decision had never been given. Arlette could not follow the confused marchings and countermarchings of that war-shadowed April. It was doubtful, indeed, if anyone had a clear picture of what was happening at any given moment. By the time messengers arrived, armies had marched on and places had changed hands again.

She knew, from the table talk at Kenilworth, that

the barons' forces were organized in three columns, commanded by the earl and his two eldest sons, Henry and Simon. She never forgot the day when an exhausted rider galloped in from Northampton. The Lord Edward had stormed the town. Its defender, young Simon, had been captured.

"I do not worry, so long as he is not badly hurt," said the countess.

"Some of the Lord Edward's men behaved like savages!" pointed out one of her ladies with round eyes.

"The common people are sure to suffer. But Edward and Simon are cousins. Simon will be treated with chivalry."

Arlette kept quiet. So, she reflected, the common people could be butchered in a quarrel that did not concern them, whereas the rival generals, if not actually struck down in fair fight, could depend on respectful treatment afterward, whether they won or lost.

The elder Simon was at this time far away in Kent. Soon news filtered through. He had captured Rochester.

"I understand," said Arlette maliciously, "that even the cathedral was plundered. The earl's men stabled their horses in it. Quite a number of the monks were murdered."

"This is war," she was told haughtily. "Even the finest general cannot always control his men after a great victory."

May brought dismal news. The earl had smashed the king's army at Lewes in Sussex, taken the king and the Lord Edward prisoner, and was at last complete master of England.

66

8

Captive Leopard

SIMON CAME TO LONDON within a fortnight of his triumph and received a wild welcome from the citizens. With him came Henry, still king in name but a helpless prisoner, compelled to agree to whatever was demanded. Three men formed the real government—Simon, young Gilbert de Clare with his great earldom of Gloucester, and Stephen de Berksted, Bishop of Chichester.

With them, too, came another royal prisoner, and now at last Michael set eyes on the Lord Edward.

More than once, walking in the unfinished abbey church at Westminster, he had stared curiously at a handsome boy's head, carved in stone. "That's the Lord Edward," one of the craftsmen had told him. "Ten years ago that was done, when he was no older than you."

Now that boy lived only in the carving. The bright flaxen hair had darkened until now, within a few weeks of his twenty-fifth birthday, it was almost black. The good looks remained. Edward was tall and athletic—one of his nicknames was "Longshanks." He was often compared with a leopard because of his rashness—that rashness that had led him too far in his cavalry charge at Lewes and had helped to give final victory to the barons. It was as a leopard that Michael saw him, a handsome, royal creature, caged but dangerous.

"But," said Hugo, "the Lord Edward was not taken prisoner. He gave himself up after the battle, as a hostage."

"Why ever did he do that?" Michael asked.

"The king was at Earl Simon's mercy. The Lord Edward does not always agree with his father, but he is a devoted son. As the earl would not trust the king and demanded hostages, he surrendered for his father's sake."

"What happens now, Hugo?"

The clerk shrugged his shoulders. "Whatever happens, the king's government goes on. Some kind of agreement was made at Lewes, but there will have to be a more permanent settlement. Meanwhile, lest the king's friends make trouble—especially the Lords Marcher on the Welsh border—Simon will keep a sharp eye on Edward. Young Henry de Montfort is to be his jailer."

"How strange! When they're cousins!"

Hugo chuckled. "You are very young, Michael, and you have enjoyed a happy family life. Relatives are not necessarily friends. Indeed, in royal circles, frequently not. But Edward and Henry get on well. They played together as children. That does not mean Henry will take any less care of his valuable prisoner, but he will not be unpleasant about it. This is no affair of chains and dungeons."

Michael soon had proof that Henry was taking no chances with his captive. The very next day he was called aside by his master. The constable looked grave.

"Well, Michael, it seems we are to part company."

"Are we, sir? I am sorry."

"So am I. You have been a good boy. You know your work, unlike some of these idle scamps. Still, there it is . . . it seems that your services are required elsewhere."

"Elsewhere, sir?"

"Certain changes are being made in the Lord Edward's personal attendants." The constable coughed meaningly. "Sir Henry feels it would be better if some of those who have been with the Lord Edward in the past were now replaced by strangers."

"I understand, sir." Michael looked the constable squarely in the eyes. "He is not to have anyone he can trust—anyone who might help him to escape."

"Sh! What romantic notions! Well, Michael, it has been suggested you might become the Lord Edward's page."

"*I*, sir? Are you serious?"

"Why not?"

"But— the king's son!"

"Do not flatter yourself, my boy. You have been chosen for the sole reason that *nothing* is known about you. You are not linked with any of the great families. You are, from Sir Henry's point of view, an extremely safe choice."

"I understand, sir," said Michael steadily. "Compared with a De Clare or a Mortimer, I am . . . a nobody."

"In these days," said the constable, "that is a very comfortable thing to be."

It was not, however, so very comfortable at first, taking over the new duties that had been imposed upon him.

"The new page, are you?" growled the boy he was to replace. "Or should I say the spy?"

Michael clenched his fists. It was all he could do to restrain himself. But, when he saw the tears of anger gleaming in the other boy's eyes, he said gently, "I can't help this, any more than you can."

"I—I suppose not. I'm sorry."

Michael waited a moment, then went on in a lighter tone. "Look, I realize I can't hope to look after him as well as you have—but it won't help matters if I'm worse than I need be. Won't you show me how he likes things done? After all, you want him to be as comfortable as possible, don't you?"

The departing page pulled himself together. He showed Michael the Lord Edward's clothes, hanging on pegs or neatly folded in a press. Michael was struck by their plainness. These simple homespun garments might have belonged to a workman rather than to the king's son.

"But that's just like him," explained the other page. "I've seen him turn to and work with his own hands, when every man was needed on the fortifications. And when our supplies were cut off by floods, in the Welsh campaign, he'd only eat the same rations as the men. He'd just one cask of wine, but he gave it to be divided, as far as it'd go."

70

"He sounds very fair."

"Fair! I should say he is. He apologized to me once —he'd clouted me, you see, over something he thought I'd done. You have to watch out when he's in a rage, that's the only trouble with him. Well, he found out afterward that he'd been in the wrong. And he apologized, just as though I were his equal. Not many masters would do that."

"No," Michael agreed thoughtfully. Now that he had seen the Lord Edward's powerful physique, he would do his best to avoid both the clout and the apology.

Within an hour Michael knew a great deal, not only about his new master's wardrobe, armor, horses, saddles, and taste in food but also about his character.

"You may have to play chess with him," he was warned. "He doesn't care much for books, but he *is* fond of music. He likes pretty well all kinds of sport —hunting and hawking, and you'll have heard how keen he is on tournaments. Horse races, too." The page chuckled at a sudden memory. "I remember once when he persuaded the royal laundress to take part in one of them! He's got a real sense of humor." He ran a polishing cloth over one of the helmets. The hauberks were like shirts of glittering dragon hide, each overlapped iron ring a point of light. "Keep his armor clean," he said with a sudden fervor. "Heaven knows when he'll be able to wear it again. But he will!"

"Of course he will!"

"I think that's everything, then. You'd better come along and be presented, I suppose."

Edward was alone. He was sitting in front of a

chessboard, thoughtfully contemplating the ivory pieces, as though busy with some secret calculation. His great head lifted as the boys came in, and Michael saw that same droop of the left eyelid which he had noticed in King Henry.

"Well?" he growled. Michael was duly introduced, dropping on one knee. "Vallier? I remember your f-father at court when I was a b-boy." He had a slight hesitation in his speech at times, though, when necessary, he could talk eloquently in either French or English. "You play chess?" He turned abruptly to the board. "If you were white, in this s-situation, how would you defend your king?"

Michael jumped to his feet and studied the pieces. Then moving one of the knights, he said: "I would attack, my lord, like this."

"And suppose black counters with his bishop, *so*?"

"That would not matter." Michael's hand flickered over the board again, lifting one of the carved pieces.

"No more it would!" said Edward with a grunt of appreciation. Once absorbed in the problem, he lost his stammer. He picked up a castle.

"Excuse me, my lord. I can take your castle—thus —which I *think*—" Michael paused tactfully.

"Gives you the game!" Edward finished the sentence for him. "Beautiful mate, my boy." The moodiness had gone from voice and eyes, he glowed with enthusiasm. "You have the right idea of it. A boy who can play chess can do other things." He stood up, laying an immense hand on the shoulder of the other page. "My young friend here knows that I would not willingly part from him. But he knows, too, that I must not hold that to your disadvantage. I take men as I find them, Michael Vallier, and that goes for boys as well. Play fair with me, and I shall play fair with you." He paused. "Y-you are w-willing to serve me?"

"Yes, my lord," said Michael huskily. In that first brief encounter the captive leopard had taken a captive of his own.

That midsummer, Kenilworth saw much activity. Fresh troops arrived to strengthen the garrison.

"Are we expecting an attack?" Arlette inquired of the countess.

"Oh, no, dear. Though everything is so upset, one cannot be too careful. Some of the king's friends have not really accepted the new arrangements—they seem very restless, over in the Welsh marches, but they would hardly dare to strike at Kenilworth."

"Then what is happening? I saw a cartload of fresh rushes being brought in—there's a great sweeping going on in the hall."

"I was going to tell you. Henry is arriving tonight. He's bringing my nephew with him."

"The Lord Edward?" Arlettes' eyes opened wider with pleasure. "How wonderful!"

"I don't know about 'wonderful,' " said the countess grimly. "It may be somewhat embarrassing. Edward is . . . not free. However, that is the men's affair. We must behave just as though everything were as usual. We must remember that he is, after all, the king's son."

"I shall not forget it, madam," Arlette answered pointedly. "*Some* people may need a reminder."

The countess shrugged her shoulders and rustled away to supervise the preparations. Really, she thought, she had enough trials without this chit of a girl continually irritating everybody. She would be thankful when the Roman lawyers gave their verdict, dissolving the first Renfield marriage, so that Arlette de la Garde could be taken off her hands.

It was early evening when a distant trumpet call, answered by the watchman's horn, announced that the party was riding through the town. Instantly the bustle within the castle was redoubled. Grooms appeared from the stables. Like swallows gathering to migrate, the ladies began to cluster on the steps of the hall.

The drawbridge rumbled like a long-drawn roll of far-off thunder. Now, with a jingle of harness, the first horsemen broke into the sunlit inner bailey. Arlette searched their faces eagerly. Henry de Montfort she knew. Ah, that tall one beside him must be the Lord Edward, and beside him again another royal hostage, his cousin, Henry of Almaine . . . and—good heavens! Who was that page just behind them? Not —*not* Michael Vallier?

Surely she knew that face under the slashed fringe of hair! He had grown since they had parted at Leicester, but he was the same boy. And that was his dear old Sorelle he was riding—Sorelle who had often nuzzled her own hand for tidbits. What were they doing here?

Michael's eyes met hers. There was no look of recognition in them. Arlette's smile froze. It *was* Michael. He must remember her—he knew she was at Kenilworth, he would be expecting to see her; there was no excuse for that cold, stranger's stare.

If he imagines he can treat me like this, she thought, he is much mistaken! I suppose he has done very well for himself, getting in with the De Montforts—the winning side!

9

Master and Page

MISUNDERSTANDINGS WERE VERY WELL, Arlette considered, in ballads. In real life, between sensible people who had once been friends, they were just foolish. If they could be removed by the speaking of a few direct words, the sooner those words were spoken, the better.

When she learned that Michael was page to the Lord Edward, and not to any of his captors, she began to think she might have misjudged him. Another thought occurred to her, also. Would it not be much better for them to meet as apparent strangers? Unless reminded, the countess would scarcely connect this new page with the youth who had written to Arlette all those months ago; but if she did, she would try to prevent their seeing anything of each other.

It was therefore vital to get a few moments alone with Michael and explain matters, before he mentioned to any of the Kenilworth household that he had met her before.

It was not difficult, amid all the confusion of that first evening, with newly arrived knights and squires and pages asking their way along unfamiliar passages, to pluck Michael by the sleeve and draw him into a quiet corner.

"Well?" he said calmly, looking down at her.

"What's the matter, Michael? You knew I'd be here."

"Yes."

"Then why did you stare right through me?"

"It is for the lady to acknowledge the gentleman first," he answered stiffly, "and to show if she wishes to renew the acquaintance. Especially when she has previously failed to reply to his letter."

"Oh, don't talk like a manual on etiquette!" she said impatiently. "There was a very good reason why I didn't reply—I was not allowed to. It wasn't considered proper. So there's no need to stand on your dignity."

"Splendid!" Michael's face broke into a smile. "I did hope there'd be some explanation. But I meant to wait and see what you did. I didn't want you to think I was . . . well, trying to make something out of our knowing each other before. I mean, it was only by accident we ever met. And I'm still very much of a nobody, and likely to stay so—the barony looks farther away than ever. I say," he added, "you've grown up since Nottingham! That's another thing, you look such a grand young lady—"

"Do I?" she said delightedly.

"I had a job to pick you out, among all the others on the steps."

"But you did!"

"Oh, yes. But what I mean is—" He paused awkwardly. "You'll be getting married quite soon, won't you? We're not just a boy and a girl now, scrambling about on the rocks in front of Hardraw—"

"I wish we were!" she burst out.

"But we're not. We're grown up—nearly—and we've got to behave accordingly."

"I know." She nodded gravely. "If people notice that we are friendly, they'll start gossiping. And the countess will lecture me again. No. We must see each other —I've a hundred things to ask you, Michael, and I've no real friends here. It's hateful. But we must be discreet." She stamped her foot viciously. "Oh, how I hate discretion!"

Michael laughed. "Then we'd better not stay here. Someone's sure to see us."

"Look out for me tomorrow morning, in the crowd. I'll drop something, so you can pick it up and speak to me. We must act rather stiffly, but we can have quite a talk, just the same."

The terms of the Lord Edward's captivity were not hard. He was free to move about the castle and take exercise outside—but always under escort. He could even ride in the forest. He could receive visitors in his private chamber. Only, if they were important personages, coming on state matters, or old friends who might be dangerous to the barons, Henry de Montfort took care to be present. Otherwise, the tower in which the hostages were lodged was treated as a suite of royal apartments, in which they were guests rather than prisoners.

It was thus quite easy for Arlette and Michael to meet the next day, when a great party rode out hawking before dinner. She was not the only girl to pair off with one of the new arrivals from London, and, if the countess noticed, she said nothing. After months of quiet country life, it was natural for everyone to want news of the outside world.

"What is he like?" she whispered.

"The Lord Edward?"

"Of course! I've always wondered. I used to think of him as a hero of romance—Roland or Sir Galahad."

"He *is* like that, in some ways," Michael admitted cautiously. "He's very strong. I've seen him just lay one hand on his horse and jump straight into the saddle. He must have terrific muscles."

Arlette listened with interest. In one way, of course, the Lord Edward was disqualified as a hero of romance—he was married, with a baby daughter. On the other hand, being separated from his Spanish princess and their offspring, he acquired an extra pathos. Arlette decided to be realistic. She put aside the daydream of being this hero's bride. She was ten years too late. A new idea presented itself. What nobler object could she have in life, what more unselfish scheme could she evolve than to arrange Edward's escape from captivity and restore him to his sorrowing wife and child? She broached the idea to Michael, in an undertone, at a moment when everyone else was tracking the flight of a falcon.

"We could ask him," was Michael's somewhat discouraging reply. He was aware of the difficulties involved.

However, Arlette would not rest until an opportunity was made to present her to the Lord Edward in his chamber.

"You see," she explained candidly, "I might be of use to you, my lord. I know you can trust Michael—but there are things I can do which Michael can't. I live here—he's a stranger, and, what's more, he *is* your page. They'd suspect him. You're not laughing at me, my lord?"

"C-certainly not, my dear. P-proceed."

"I haven't thought out any details, yet. I know how closely watched you are when you go out."

"I am most honorably attended," Edward admitted with a bitter smile.

"Your only chance to get away is in some kind of disguise. Perhaps in women's clothes. That's where I could help."

Edward burst out laughing. He looked at Arlette's slenderness. He spread his great arms and shook with helpless amusement.

"I don't mean mine, my lord," she said, a trifle nettled. "I could borrow something much bigger."

"I beg your pardon." He was grave again immediately. "My dear, I must explain to you. First, let me say how much I appreciate your offer. Do you understand how serious the consequences might be to yourself?"

"I am prepared to take them." Her chin tilted in a gesture Michael remembered.

"So be it. None the less, I cannot accept your sacrifice. I am not—as things are—in a position to escape."

"But why not, my lord?"

"I am here as a hostage. I have had to make a bargain for my father's sake. Henry de Montfort need not guard me when I g-go riding in the forest. I would consider myself dishonored if I ran away. Y-you understand?"

"Yes, my lord," she answered in a flat tone. It was disappointing, blackly disappointing; but, if his word had been given, she would not have had him behave differently. Honor mattered more than anything in the world. She clutched at a remnant of hope. "Is there anything that you feel free to do?" she begged. "If you wanted a secret message taken to any of your friends—"

"You would have it sent?" he asked with a keen glance.

She shook her head. "I have no one I can send with letters—Michael knows that. But if it were really important I would take it myself."

"Yourself!"

"I can ride as hard as most men," she said with dignity. "I'd dress as a boy, then nobody would stop me. I'd ride from here to the Welsh border if you wanted!"

He studied her in silence. "I believe you would," he said. "And if ever the need arises, I shall not hesitate to ask you."

"But not now, my lord?"

"N-not now. Not yet."

The royal leopard would not submit to be caged forever. Michael assured Arlette of that when they had their next chance to talk together. After weeks of close daily contact with Edward, he felt he could judge his character.

Edward had taken to his new page. Michael's skill at chess had forged the first bond of common interest between them. But it proved to be neither the only one nor the most important.

Edward was struck by the boy's unusual knowledge of public business, taught him by Hugo Best. He himself, as a youth, had been tutored in law by another Chancery clerk, Robert Burnell. Michael was a boy after his own heart. One day, when fortune smiled, he might be able to do something for him.

Michael told him about his claim. The case was still dragging on. Edward nodded.

"I know. There is a great deal wrong with the courts of this country. Justice is slow—and not even sure. That must all be changed." He looked hard at Michael. "A time will come when *I* shall have a say in these matters. I do not promise you the Grevel barony—it may not be your right, and you cannot be favored because you have served me well. But whatever is right, that you shall have."

That was what Michael admired in his master. His fairness. Once, Edward had stupefied him by saying that there was wisdom in some of Simon's ideas. It would be right, for instance, to widen the membership of the Great Council. Knights should be chosen from every shire to discuss affairs with the barons; merchants, too, now that the towns were growing more important—after all, their taxes made up more and more of the king's revenue.

"Years ago," Edward confessed, "I almost fell out with my dear father over that kind of thing. He accused me of becoming a De Montfort supporter myself!" He laughed. "It seems strange now. But, as I say, some of the earl's ideas are good. It is his way of working for them that I like less and less. The king's authority must not be weakened." He thumped the table till the chessmen rocked. "The king is all the common man understands. Changes must come through the king, not by rebellion against him."

Michael liked it when Edward could be led on to speak of his own boyhood. He had been born at Westminster and, until he was seven, had spent most of his time at Windsor.

He was very fond of his father. He remembered standing on the shore and watching the ship that carried him away to Gascony. "I was fourteen then," he admitted, "but I cried till the ship was only a black point on the skyline." Then he laughed. "A year later I was sailing off to join him, and then I was at the Spanish court at Burgos, kneeling before King Alfonso to be knighted."

"That must have been wonderful."

"It is the moment one must never forget. And two months later—I was just fifteen—I married his young half sister. I can see it all now, the dark church at Las Huelgas, King Alfonso, all the other faces . . . except hers." Again he laughed. "I was too nervous, I suppose."

He had spent the rest of that year, and most of the next, serving in Gascony, where he first came into conflict with his uncle, Earl Simon.

"He was more at home there than I was. He's French, I'm English. I believe the time has come to stop worrying about our claims on the Continent and set our own house in order. It's Wales we should turn to, not Gascony. And Scotland. That's where our future lies."

So Edward had been glad to sail home and be given the great earldom of Chester, with rights over all the royal lands in Wales, the whole of Ireland, Jersey, and

Guernsey. "It sounds like a great deal," he explained with a smile, "but it produces more trouble than revenue, Wales especially. One day, I shall take the country in hand. Castles are the answer, dominating all the key points. But there are more urgent matters before I can dream of that."

Michael was silent. He was wondering whether to tell Edward what Arlette had overheard Henry de Montfort saying to his mother: that the earldom of Chester was too dangerous a power to leave in Edward's hands.

The Kenilworth visit ended all too soon. Early in August the captives were taken off to Canterbury, where the king and the earl were to make a final settlement.

When Edward returned from the conference his eyes were like coals. He paced his chamber furiously, and Michael did not dare to open his mouth until spoken to. At last Edward burst out:

"I was a fool not to take that girl's offer at Kenilworth! But I don't know . . . I feel now my hands are free."

"What has happened, my lord?" Michael ventured.

"A settlement. To be called the P-peace of Canterbury!" Edward's scorn was terrible. "My father to be a mere figurehead—no more than the seal to be stamped on Simon's orders! Why did he submit? Because he could not face the alternative. Do you know what that—that man threatened? Dared to threaten the king's majesty? My father to be deposed—and for me, his heir, perpetual imprisonment!"

10

Trumpets at Dawn

AFTER THE PEACE of Canterbury there was a growing awkwardness between captive and captors.

Edward was still treated with courtesy. Henry de Montfort was clearly uncomfortable in his role of jailer, but he obeyed his father's orders to the letter. He seemed to feel that Edward was behaving unreasonably. Surely this miserable dispute between their parents was over! Why couldn't they go back to their old friendship?

Edward's temper was difficult, even Michael admitted that. Though so far he had escaped physical punishment, he had suffered his share of curses and criticisms. Sometimes Edward apologized later, and sometimes not.

Leopards were not born for cages, that was the truth of it. Edward was a man of tremendous energy, fretting because he could not use it. Also, though free from vanity, he was proud—he was not prepared to bow his head to any man other than his own father and king.

Much to Michael's disappointment, they did not go back to Kenilworth. Instead, they were taken to Wallingford, where a castle guarded one of the main crossings of the Thames. It belonged to Edward's uncle, Earl Richard, so-called King of the Romans, but he too had been taken prisoner at the Battle of Lewes.

Michael was learning to study each of their fresh lodgings in turn: what were the possibilities of escape? He had to admit that they were not good. There were three moats to cross, apart from the intervening walls. The innermost moat enclosed the keep on its mound and the great hall; a second moat ran around the other bailey, and a third encircled the whole town of Wallingford. On the north side all three moats ran close together and parallel. All were fed from the Thames, which lay below the walls and bastions to the east.

That, for a strong swimmer, would be the most promising escape route. Even then, there would be difficulties. To dive from the battlements might mean a broken neck—the walls were high, the depth of the river unknown. A long rope would be needed, and there was no chance of getting one unless they could bribe one of De Montfort's men.

"And then—what?" said Edward, when Michael brought up the subject. "Suppose I got across to the Oxfordshire side—unarmed, half naked, no horse, with Sir Henry rousing the whole countryside to hunt me down! There is no safety for me nearer than the Welsh Marches. I couldn't get as far as Oxford." He faced Michael. "You don't imagine I'm afraid?"

"Of course not, my lord!"

"I have more than myself to think of. I am the king's son, and the king too is a prisoner, and too old to fight, anyhow." No older than Simon, thought Michael, but he did not say so. Edward was right on the main point. Any effective resistance to the barons would come from himself, not from his father. It was a question of character rather than age. "When I escape," Edward continued, "I must not be recaptured. You understand? Because there may be no second chance. There must be no mistake about it."

"But, my lord, you must have so many friends outside; if only we could get into touch with them—"

"The Wool Merchant sees we don't," said Edward.

That was the latest nickname for Henry de Montfort. For a time, he had been governor of the Cinque Ports, the southern maritime towns controlling the cross-Channel trade with France. The earl's new government had put a ban on the export of English wool. Henry had enforced it so strictly that people accused him of seizing the wool for his own profit. Hence the nickname, and it gave Edward great pleasure to use it when he was angry.

No, the Wool Merchant was taking no chances with his royal cousin. No secret messages got past his censorship. Edward could only guess at what was happening in other parts of the country. Two things appeared certain: that the king was completely in the earl's power, but that by no means every man obeyed the orders that Simon issued in his name. In the wilder regions of England, where powerful barons sat secure in their fortresses, a law to themselves, there was plenty of opposition to the De Montfort rule. It needed time to organize—and it needed a leader.

So Edward bided his time. He played chess with his fellow prisoner and favorite cousin, Henry of Almaine, and with Michael. He paced the battlements, watching the autumn colors change day by day in the Chiltern beechwoods across the river. He spent patient hours coaching the boy in the use of sword and dagger, or talking about the art of fortification, which fascinated him.

"Castles must change," he would say, and his stammer would disappear as it always did when he was most interested. "We need to push the outer walls— the curtains—farther from the heart of the fortress. That's to keep the enemy's archers at a safer distance. The range is getting longer than it was years ago. The longbow's a better weapon than the crossbow —I've found that out, fighting the Welsh. It may drive out the crossbow in the end. If we improve it enough, and make it still longer and more powerful, it may alter things on the open battlefield too."

Michael learned from him that the main function of moats was to prevent besieging sappers from undermining the walls at the base. For the attackers, the best thing to do with moats was to drain them—if you had the time and the man power.

"We might be able to do that at a place like Kenilworth," said Edward, "and someday, perhaps, we shall have the pleasure of trying! It's an artificial lake there. If we broke the dam at one end, it would all run out."

"That couldn't be done here, my lord. Fresh water would keep running in from the river."

"Yes. The best way to take Wallingford would be a surprise attack."

Autumn passed. Dank mists rose from the Thames and wreathed into every corner of the castle. Michael wondered how long this life would continue. Soon it would be Christmas, and he felt homesick for Hardraw. It was eighteen months and more since he had seen his family.

It was not that he weakened for a moment in his loyalty to the Lord Edward. But, oh, it would have been good to see the weather-bitten crags of Raven's Edge against the sky instead of the man-made battlements of Wallingford, and to change this oily, sluggish Thames for the jumping, bustling rivers of home!

Their stay at Wallingford came to a sudden end a week or two before Christmas.

Michael, snuggled down under the bedclothes with Godfrey, who was Henry of Almaine's page, woke abruptly and sat up in the icy grayness of the December dawn. What was that? Again. . . . Who was blowing trumpets at this hour of the morning? Who had arrived?

Men were shouting. Heavy footsteps clattered over the paving stones below. There was the clink of mail, the rattle of a dropped shield sliding and bumping down the stairs. Then once more that strident, heart-quickening bray of trumpets!

Godfrey stirred. Sleepily he tugged at the coverlet and wriggled the shoulder which Michael had left bare by sitting upright. Michael gave him a poke.

"Rouse yourself! Something's happening!"

"Michael!" That was the Lord Edward bellowing. "What have you done with my shoes?"

Michael pattered across the rush-strewn floor. In the dim light filtering through the window slits, Edward loomed hugely before him, tucking his shirt into his hose. He snatched the shoes.

89

"Those swords they let us have for practice, yesterday—did they go back?"

"Yes, my lord. They always lock them up again, with your armor."

Edward swore. "Not so much as a dagger! Are you there, Harry?" Henry of Almaine came through the curtained doorway. "I don't know who it is—it must be some of our friends. From the shouting, I think they've reached the outer bailey. Only a moat and a wall between us! We must do something."

He snatched up a stool and weighed it in his hands.

"What can we do but wait?" said his fellow prisoner more calmly. "We can't get at our arms."

"If we could get the key to where they are! Or batter down the door— is it a heavy door, Michael?"

"Very, my lord. And it opens outward."

"Then we must arm ourselves from the enemy." Edward brandished the stool. Henry of Almaine protested.

"And give them the excuse they need to finish you?"

"I c-can't do nothing—listening to that noise outside."

As he spoke, the tumult swelled. They could hear the brisk rattle and thud of arrows, and voices bawling orders against a confused background of cheers.

Then, even as they listened, trying to distinguish the course of the battle, armed feet came clattering up their own staircase. Edward drew back from the doorway, his stool poised to strike. He lowered it hopelessly as half a dozen mail-clad figures came crowding in. The foremost was Henry de Montfort.

"Edward—"

90

"Well?"

"Some of your friends are outside. They took us by surprise. They were through the town and into the outer defenses before we knew they were there—"

"Excellent! You *must* have been . . . woolgathering."

"You are not out of the wood yet," young De Montfort reminded him. "You had better come out on the battlements and speak to them."

"Who are they?"

"Warren de Bassingburne seems to be there—"

"Ah, my old comrade in Gascony. Who else?"

"Robert Waleran—"

"I thought he was a hundred miles away at least."

"So did we," said De Montfort grimly. "They were in Wales. They must have come on broomsticks! Come along." He motioned them to the door. "This is serious, Edward," he warned him. "Cousin or no cousin . . . if you try any tricks, I shall treat you as I would anyone else."

They all went up on to the battlements. A red wintry sun was rising over the frosted ridge of the Chilterns. Its rusty beams glowed on the iron caps and chain-mail hauberks of the men lining the wall. Some of them, Michael noticed, were winding the capstan of a mangonel, a giant catapult he had been studying a few days before. Inch by inch the beam was hauled back into a horizontal position, when the spoon-shaped end was ready for loading. It was a wicked-looking contraption. As the men grunted at their work and the thing squeaked and groaned with the increasing tension, he realized for the first time what a terrifying force was imprisoned in that skein of twisted sinew.

"Sound the trumpet for a parley," ordered De Montfort.

The trumpet rang out and was quickly answered from below. The shouting died down, the whir and rattle of arrows ceased. He turned to Edward. "Are you prepared to speak to them?"

"It depends."

"You might as well understand this—and make them understand it, too. They have been very lucky so far. They'll get no farther, without siege equipment." He hurried on, "They can't sit down in front of the castle indefinitely. My father will come to relieve us. They won't be able to stand up against him."

"Shall we wait and see?" said Edward with a smile.

"No. Listen, Edward. You see that mangonel?"

"Yes."

"Your friends outside have been howling for you to be sent out to them. Very well. If they don't go away—immediately—you *shall* be sent, but not in a way that you will appreciate!" He pointed to the giant catapult. It was now fully cocked. But there was nothing in the holder.

Edward swallowed. In a low, stifled voice he said: "I knighted you. . . ."

"That has nothing to do with it. I said, 'cousin or no cousin.' I hold this castle, and I mean to hold it."

Henry of Almaine stepped forward. "This is barbarity—"

"This is war. Edward, you can tell your friends to go away, or, by all that's holy, I'll send you to join them!"

Edward was silent for a moment. Michael stood

92

petrified with horror. Henry of Almaine laid a hand on the prince's arm, murmuring something.

"Very well," snarled Edward, "I'll speak to them, since you leave me no choice. But I shall not forget."

He sprang upon the wall and stood there, bare-headed in the sunrise, and a cheer rose from far below, changing—as his clear voice rang out in explanation—to a sullen murmur like the sea.

11

Dark Winter

GRUMBLING BUT OBEDIENT, the royalist knights withdrew their forces from the outer parts of the castle, rode through the frightened town, and headed for the safety of the west. As soon as the coast was clear, De Montfort ordered his men to get ready for the road. Christmas would be spent in his mother's fortress at Kenilworth. In the heart of his own countryside, there would be less risk of a similar raid.

Arlette was delighted to see Lord Edward and Michael again. She managed to forget for the time being how much she hated her position in the De Montfort household. She forgot, too, that the decision of the Roman law courts was expected in the new year, setting the Earl of Renfield free to marry her, and that her only chance of escape from Kenilworth was to accept a husband she did not want. For the twelve days of Christmas she remembered only that she was young.

Her clear voice pealed out with the others as they thronged the chapel, singing carols; and later in the hall, when the long tables were spread with black velvet embroidered in gold and flame, and laden with silver cups and platters winking back the light of fire and candles, she stood with the rest to welcome the procession as it entered with the boar's head steaming and glistening on its dish.

> The Boar's Head in hand bear I,
> Bedecked with bays and rosemary;
> And I pray you, my masters, be merry,
> *Quot estis in convivio.*
> *Caput apri defero,*
> *Reddens laudes Domino!*

What a banquet it was! The first course alone included roast veal, swan, peacock, crane, and venison. The second, along with the boar's head, brought nearly a dozen other meats, with glazed chicken and a mixed grill. Fortunately, the third course was a light one—a mere trifling with jellies and pastries, figs and dates, and small game like quail and pigeon. In this way a corner was left for the sweets and lumps of green ginger heaped in little bowls along the table.

The celebrations went on until Twelfth Night, when there was acting, with the pages dressing up to amuse their elders. Michael, who had a talent for that kind of thing, appeared as Hercules in a fantastic red beard and did valiant battle with a stuffed lion. Arlette, who had eaten rather too much and was wearing too close-fitting a dress in honor of the occasion, laughed so heartily that it hurt.

The next morning she woke to the realization that Christmas was gone for another year, that the blackest months of winter lay still in front, and that everybody in the castle, herself included, was a little bilious.

Next Christmas, she thought with a shiver, she might be Countess of Renfield. . . .

"What can I do?" she asked Michael.

In theory, no girl could be forced to marry against her will. In practice, it was happening all the time. Girls had no freedom. They must do what was arranged for them.

"You've only one chance," Michael told her gloomily.

"What's that?"

"If the king can throw off the earl in time."

"What a slender hope!"

"Not if the Lord Edward escapes. You said once you would help us. Are you still willing?"

"Of course!" she assured him fervently. She had been willing enough when for herself it meant only danger and sacrifice. Now she had a personal motive. Her own future depended on the overthrow of Simon's power, and Edward was the only man who could manage that.

But luck was against her. Before any scheme could be laid it was the old story—a bustle of packing, a loading of baggage animals (the winter mud was too deep for carts), a mustering of armed horsemen, and then nothing but a dark column of dwindling figures between the snow-dappled fields. Once more the prisoners were on the move. For the third time she said good-bye to Michael.

It was with a new understanding now and a far deeper interest that Arlette followed the news which reached the ladies at Kenilworth.

Earl Simon had summoned the Great Council to
meet on the twentieth of January. Parliament, people were beginning to call it, from the French *parler*,
to speak. For the first time, knights of the shires and
burgesses from the towns were to sit in conference
with their superiors.

Only a year ago, her aristocratic senses would
have revolted against the very idea. What right had
such men to meddle, however slightly, with the affairs of the kingdom? Now, after talking so much to
Michael and learning that the Lord Edward himself
agreed with it, she was only angry that Simon should
be the first to put it into practice.

Of course, she told herself, he had his reasons! He
was losing his control over his fellow barons. How
could he hope to dominate them forever when he
was no more than one of them himself—no, less
than that, a penniless foreign adventurer who had
crept into their ranks? Naturally he was looking for
fresh allies to bolster his position. It was a meeting
packed with his own supporters. Only five earls and
seventeen barons were there.

Living in a De Montfort stronghold, she found it
hard to learn what was being said on the other side.
She had to piece together such hints as came her
way. It looked as if the earl's popularity had fallen
since his triumph at Lewes. It was whispered that
complete power had spoiled him and that he was
more overbearing than ever; that, for all the talk of
his pious character, he was not above robbing the
London Jews and keeping much of the plunder for
himself; that he was favoring his sons with the gift

of lands confiscated from the king's supporters, and with offices of which they made good use. As for the pledge to clear foreigners out of the kingdom, it was noticed that some foreigners were left undisturbed; presumably those who paid for protection.

The earl's own character seemed to be against him at a time like this. The very qualities that made him so great a soldier—courage, self-confidence, a tremendous forcefulness—made it harder for him to keep his supporters together when the fighting was over.

"My lord cannot compromise," said the countess proudly. "He does nothing by halves. He cannot hide his true feelings as some people do—he has no patience with fools."

Fools being those who disagree with him, thought Arlette, bending over her needlework to hide a smile. That would be Earl Simon's undoing. But, oh, would something happen in time?

February brought a hopeful rumor. Simon had fallen out with his most powerful ally, Gilbert de Clare, Earl of Gloucester. Gilbert, only twenty-one, was conscious of his own importance. He held vast estates in twenty-two different counties, as well as in Wales and Ireland, and he was not prepared to be Simon's junior partner forever.

Would it come to anything? A real, open quarrel? Arlette knew enough of warlike matters to realize that the Gloucester domains, joined to those of the Lord Edward's supporters on the Welsh border, would form a powerful combination. But for the time being nothing happened. Gilbert de Clare had gone home.

"Sulking," said the countess. She had no doubt that he would come running out again to lick his master's hand.

Arlette relapsed into gloom. She was roused, but only for a short time, by news from London. The release of the royal hostages had been publicly proclaimed in Westminster Hall. The Lord Edward was free! Now, surely, her storybook knight would ride into action.

"Well, he is not actually *free*." The countess pursed her lips as she threaded her needle. "Matters are extremely delicate, at the moment. My nephew is such an impulsive young man—and the country so unsettled. If only for his own good, and his father's, he must be prevented from making trouble. My son Henry will continue to look after him."

"Then—that proclamation was just a lie?"

"Certainly not, child!" The countess hesitated. "I suppose you would call it a legal pronouncement. It formally puts an end to the Lord Edward's period as a hostage—"

"But he remains a prisoner!"

"Only for the time being."

Arlette snorted. "I can't see that the proclamation means a thing."

"You forget, it applies also to my other nephew, Henry of Almaine. And he has been allowed to leave the country."

"Oh, who cares about Henry of Almaine?"

She was sorry for that remark years later. Kneeling at prayer in a church at Viterbo in Italy, Henry was attacked and savagely murdered by the younger

Simon de Montfort and his brother Guy. But on that
March day in 1265 the knowledge was hidden from
her.

Michael, too, was angry when he discovered that the
Westminster proclamation was an empty form of
words, and his master was as closely guarded as
before.

"I expected no more," Edward tried to console
him. "It shows that Simon is not feeling secure. And
I would rather take my liberty than receive it as a
favor."

It was typical of Edward's kindliness that he chose
this moment to promote Michael to the position of
squire. He was old enough—there was no hard-and-
fast rule—and he deserved it. For the present it
meant very little difference to his duties. "But the
day may not be so far off," Edward warned him,
"when you have my shield to carry and my spurs to
buckle on. The signs continue good."

They did, but it took the eye of understanding to
read them. One was the retirement of the new chancellor, Thomas de Cantelupe. De Montfort supporter
though he was, he refused to be a mere pawn, fixing
the king's Great Seal to whatever document the barons laid before him.

There was a still more important development in
April when the court moved from London to North-
ampton, and Gilbert de Clare was summoned to attend.
He refused.

Edward rubbed his hands with glee. "Pull one stick
out, and the whole b-bundle will fall apart! The part-
ners begin to quarrel. Now we shall see."

Late that month Earl Simon marched to Gloucester. The king, as always, he kept at his side, and this
time he took Edward too. Thomas de Clare, Gilbert's
younger brother, had shown no signs of joining in
the dispute. In fact he was helping Henry de Montfort to guard the royal prisoner.

They were all lodged in the great abbey beside the
Severn, where, as a small boy, the king had been
crowned nearly half a century before.

Soon it would be May. Already the days were hot,
the dusk fragrant with the smell of grass and flowers
and the broad river rolling seaward. After dark they
could see the campfires on the ridges of the Forest
of Dean, reddening the sky and quenching the stars.
Gilbert de Clare's men, too few to fight yet, were
watching their chance. . . .

Another sign came. Two royalists sailed back from
exile overseas, the Earl of Surrey and William of
Valence. Having only a hundred and twenty followers, they landed in the far western safety of Pem-
brokeshire. Given time, they knew their forces would
grow. So did Earl Simon. He gave orders to march
to Hereford, where he would be better placed to
meet a threat from Wales.

"Y-you see, Michael?" said Edward exultantly. "The
dark winter is over—now for the spring!"

12

A Horse Race at Hereford

ON THE ROAD to Hereford, Michael caught his first
glimpse of the castle that might one day be his. The
walls of Grevel were of the local stone, warm and
red as the plowed fields. It stood, backed by dense
woods, on a hillock above the bustling Wye. One way
it looked to the Forest of Dean, the other to the
cloud-wreathed ridges of Brecon and Radnor. From
the battlements, he guessed, there would be a glimpse
of the Severn Sea. But the chances of ever climbing
up there to look at it were small indeed.

They spent May at Hereford, a fine walled city
with six gates, defended by the Wye. Its castle was
one of the half-dozen strongholds spaced along the
Welsh border from Chester in the north to Chepstow
in the south.

"Castles and rivers," explained the Lord Edward
to his new squire. "Those are what you must know
about if you'd play at war as well as you play at
chess."

He took a twig and drew lines in the soft earth of
the garden. He showed how the Wye, curving out of
the Welsh hills, made a defensive line which could

be held by castles at the fords and bridges. Farther east, the Severn made a second line. The northern half of the border was protected similarly by the Dee.

"You see what the earl is after? If he can hold the river crossings, he can keep Surrey and Valence penned in Wales. You can't lead armies across narrow bridges—let alone fords or ferries—when they're strongly defended on the other side. Yet you have to use the normal crossings. Armored men can't swim, and it's hard to muster enough boats in one place without the enemy's finding out."

Information, he told Michael, was the third important thing for a general. It was always a nightmare, wondering where your enemy was and where he would move next. However reliable your scouts, and however fast they rode, their reports were stale by the time they arrived.

"The most they can tell you is where the enemy *was*," he said. "You have to guess from that where he is now—and where he *will* be by the time you can take action against him. That's where rivers help again. They simplify the guesswork. There are only a few places where he can cross, so you can cut down the possibilities accordingly."

A general's memory should be stored with information about roads and distances. Local people were not always reliable. Vagueness over a few miles might lose a battle.

"It's very interesting," said Michael.

He had no desire to kill anyone, but some matters, it seemed, could be decided no other way, and one of them was, at the present moment, who should be master of England. At least one should try to make sure that it came to a quick decision, without useless, drawn-out slaughter. One knock-out blow was more merciful than a long battering. Therein, he could see, lay the fascination of strategy.

"It's *like* chess, my lord. It's so much better to win in a few moves, cleverly, than let both sides blunder on till most of their pieces are off the board."

"Yes, Michael. But"—Edward's face darkened—"you can't play at war without taking off *some* pieces. This game will never be decided while both Simon and I are left. The board won't hold the two of us."

Michael often wondered in what manner their deliverance would come, though he never doubted that one day, somehow, his master would be free. But would it be through some midnight adventure of drugged sentries and disguises, or openly, by taking of solemn oaths and the sealing of parchment promises?

When the moment for the actual attempt drew near, the plan was different from anything he had imagined. It was so simple as to be almost obvious. And so nearly obvious that it could be wrecked, up to the last minute, by the slightest suspicion on their captors' part. It depended greatly on luck, too. If any one of half a dozen details failed to work out, there would be nothing for it but to call off the attempt.

Earl Simon stayed at Hereford to hear Mass in the cathedral on Whitsunday. Then, unwilling to sit waiting any longer for his enemies, he marched into Wales to look for them. Edward was left behind, in the charge of Henry, as usual, and of Thomas de Clare.

"Michael," he said that evening, "I want you to play chess with me."

Michael got out the ivory pieces. Edward's voice was tense. His eyes were dancing. He looked more like a man getting ready for a tournament than a thoughtful chess player. And it was a strangely casual game they played, which would have puzzled any spectator.

Fortunately there were no spectators. But it was best to have some innocent occupation to cover their talk, in case they should be interrupted.

"By God's g-grace," said Edward, moving a pawn at random, "we shall be out of here b-by Thursday."

"How, my lord?"

"Thomas de Clare is on our side. He has been playing a double game to help his brother."

"That's wonderful—"

For the past month Gilbert de Clare had been flitting about the countryside like a shadow, stirring up resistance to the De Montforts and avoiding all their efforts to hinder him.

"I can count on the De Clares and the Mortimers." Edward smiled a shade scornfully. "There are conditions, but nothing I can't agree to."

"How are you going to get away? Can I help?"

"Certainly. I need you, in fact, because you're my squire and you have to lead my spare horses. Gilbert de Clare and Roger Mortimer have concocted the plan between them, and now is the time to try it. Thursday's fixed for it—by then Simon will have ridden a good distance into the hills. We don't want him back too soon."

Leaning forward across the chessboard, Edward began to whisper the details of the plan.

Michael had a flutter in his stomach when they rode out of the city that Thursday. Would the plan work? Would the men appear as promised? Would shrewd Henry let the wool be pulled over his eyes?

They rode northward in the slanting sun. Wide-marsh, just outside the city, was a favorite riding ground, and Edward wished to try the paces of a new horse that had been sent him. Michael was leading him now, a sleek black gelding built for speed rather than weight carrying, a fine hunter but too light for a fully armored rider. Michael himself was mounted on Sorelle, and praying that the wiry little mare would be up to the work ahead of her.

Besides Henry de Montfort and Thomas de Clare there were only a handful of knights. The country lay open for miles in front, the city was close at their backs. There was no hint of danger in the neighborhood, and Henry was not worrying. These rides, under escort, were an almost daily routine. He was thankful to see his cousin harmlessly occupied. It was far better than quarreling over politics.

As they rode, Thomas de Clare started the discussion on horses, as had been carefully planned.

"For sheer ease of motion, Edward, I doubt if your new mount will come up to this mare of mine."

"I should like to try her," said Edward.

"Do, by all means."

"May I?" He tossed the reins to Michael, who sat there on Sorelle, a riderless horse on either side of him. De Clare dismounted, Edward climbed into the saddle and rode gently up and down, trying the mare in various gaits but being careful, Michael noticed, not to tire her.

This led to some brisk discussion about the finer points of horsemanship. All the knights were keen riders and proud of their own mounts. Several begged him to try theirs. Finally, at De Clare's prompting, Henry said that his cousin was very welcome to try his.

"I can see she moves well," said Edward provokingly, "but I have my doubts about her speed."

"Try her!"

"Why not a race?" put in De Clare quickly, and the suggestion was taken up by the knights. "Let Edward ride yours," he went on with a laugh, "and you ride his!"

"Which—the new one?" asked Henry, smiling.

"Not for a hundred pounds!" Edward retorted. "I haven't tried him myself yet. This young fellow will give you a good gallop."

He swung around to pat the muzzle of his other mount, before offering the reins to his cousin. His eyes went to Michael's. Michael nodded slightly. He had been keeping a sharp eye on a nearby hilltop. He had seen the mounted figure he was waiting for, and had passed on the signal to De Clare. Everything was ready.

"Which way shall we race?" Edward inquired innocently.

107

"Oh, toward the city," said Henry with automatic caution. "Your squire can stay here and be judge and finishing post as well."

The whole party wheeled their horses and trotted across the open common, but after a moment De Clare slowed down, dismounted, and began to examine the off foreleg of his mare. "Count me out this time," he called.

"Don't say I've lamed her!" Edward shouted over his shoulder, but did not turn back. Michael waited till he could see that they were all ready and roughly in line, then dropped his arm as a starting signal.

This was the moment. . . . The drumming of his heart seemed as loud as the hooves upon the sun-baked earth . . . nearer and nearer—Edward and Henry racing neck and neck, the rest strung out in the rear. What did it matter who won, so long as every horse was blown and breathless?

Michael leaned over and patted the new gelding's neck. The beast was restless, straining to be in the race.

"Steady," the boy murmured. "Your turn's coming."

The riders came at him out of a tawny dust cloud. "I think—I—win!" gasped Henry, plunging past. It was true, for Edward had begun to slacken pace before the finish, so that he could rein up beside his squire. As the other knights went by, he was out of the saddle and, in a twinkling, astride the fresh horse.

"Thanks, Michael! Come on!" he cried, and they shot forward knee to knee.

13

The Leopard Loose!

Too LATE Henry realized what was happening.

"Stop!" he bellowed. Then, as De Clare remounted and rode across the course of the fugitives: "Stop them, Thomas! Use your sword, man!"

But Thomas made no attempt to do so. Nor did his horse show any sign of the lameness that had kept him out of the race. He wheeled in behind Edward and Michael and galloped after them. Henry swore frenziedly.

"He's in it with them! I'll have his head for this! Quick, one of you—a crossbow—who's brought a crossbow? Let them have it!"

One of the knights took rapid aim and pulled the trigger. The bolt sailed through the air, but the three figures went bobbing away across the common un-harmed. Henry spurred savagely after them, but it was hopeless. His horse was blown. So were all the others. They had been tricked. And now a cluster of figures had appeared on the hilltop in front, riding to meet Edward. He recognized the Earl of Glouces-ter's colors. His heart sank.

"We'd better ride back and give the alarm," he said wearily. "Though they'll be miles away before we can get after them."

The royal leopard had broken loose. Henry wondered how he was going to tell his father.

"What now? Which way?" Edward asked eagerly, when he had answered the greeting of De Clare's knights.

"To Wigmore, first," said Thomas. "If my brother is not there with Mortimer, there will be a message for us."

It was an easy ride, for the old Roman Watling Street ran straight as a lance, mile after mile. Edward went in front with Thomas and the leader of the knights. Michael could catch only odd phrases of their talk. His master, he could tell, was pouring out shrewd questions, already planning the campaign that should free his father, smash the De Montfort party, and wipe out the disgrace of Lewes.

Nobody said much to Michael. But he was content to feel Sorelle beneath him and to know the joy of riding fast in the sunshine, under the blossoming boughs of early summer, and know that he was free.

The escape from Hereford was only the beginning of a long and dangerous road, which might easily lead to captivity again, perhaps to death. Edward and Henry de Montfort could never meet again as cousins and boyhood friends. All that was finished. It was grim war now.

But it was hard to remember such things on a golden day like this, with furry white tufts of cloud

110

swimming slowly across a blue sky and all the beauty of May just merging into the glory of June.

On they rode, sometimes through hamlets with fields of shimmering young corn, sometimes across commons where lonely shepherd boys jumped up to stare, sometimes through thorny wastelands and shadowy woods. When they came to the mill at the crossing of the River Arrow, they paused to rinse the dust from their throats with some of the miller's ale. They felt safer with the river behind them.

A little farther on, at Mortimer's Cross, they were in friendly country. For a mile they rode beside the Lugg, flowing through a gap in the steep wooded hills which rose in front of them. Then they were across that river, too, and there was Wigmore Castle on its green spur, the battlements crowded with waving figures.

Roger Mortimer's wife was there to welcome Edward. She apologized for her husband's absence, but, she added, he was busy in the king's service not far away.

The next day, Edward and Michael crossed the wild range of Bringewood Chase, to meet Mortimer and Gilbert de Clare at the great stronghold of Ludlow. There Edward made his bargain with the two barons. He promised that the old laws and charters of England would be kept, and foreigners would no longer be allowed to take the best positions in Church and state. Both sides swore solemn oaths before the altar.

And on the next day, May 30, the news of the escape reached Earl Simon's camp in Wales. He knew

111

at once what it meant. Before sunset, messengers were thundering along the roads, north, south, and east into England, carrying a proclamation in the king's name.

Every baron was to mobilize his men, and ride with all speed to an assembly point at Worcester.

When the proclamation reached Kenilworth, it was all Arlette could do to restrain herself from dancing with joy. The De Montforts—to her surprise and vexation—seemed very little worried.

"Edward was always so hotheaded," remarked the countess, shaking her head. "Such a foolish thing to do, just when everything was settling down. . . ." She held out her embroidery and studied it at arm's length. "His father will be so angry. And the earl will have something to say to poor Henry. He should never have allowed this to happen. They were always such friends as boys."

Arlette looked at her without a word. Was she really such a fool—so blind? Or was she so torn between her two family loyalties that she dared not show her feelings? That must be it, surely. . . . A great lady, keeping up appearances to the outside world, pretending that all was well when everything was rushing headlong to ruin.

The other ladies were more outspoken. Edward had put himself in the wrong. By running away and joining the "rebel" barons, as they called them, he had defied his father. Now he must be dealt with, and his uncle would be the man to deal with him. The earl had won at Lewes and he would win again. Who could stand against him?

As the days passed, however, it looked as though it might not be so simple.

Edward had been thinking ahead when he gave Michael his lesson on the importance of rivers. Now he was practicing what he had taught. With Henry de Montfort at Hereford and Earl Simon marching back, there was no hope of holding the east bank of the Wye. But the Severn was a different matter. He gave swift, decisive orders. Parties of knights and archers rode off to make sure of every bridge and ford and ferry along the river. All the bridges near Worcester were to be broken down.

On June 7 Simon faced the uncomfortable truth. He could not cross the Severn. He was barred from all the rest of England. Worcester, which he had chosen as the concentration point for his own forces, had become headquarters for Edward. He was forced to send out an altered proclamation, changing the meeting place to Gloucester. Before it could be obeyed, Edward had seized that city too, and destroyed its bridge.

What mockery, thought Arlette, when she caught sight of the parchment that came to Kenilworth. "Henry by the grace of God King of England," it began, "Lord of Ireland and Duke of Aquitaine . . ." As though the poor king had any say in the orders that carried his seal! Proud titles, but empty words. . . . It would be truer if they had read: "Henry by the favor of Earl Simon king in name only . . ."

Did he even see the documents issued for him? She could not believe it. Especially when a proclamation followed declaring the Lord Edward a rebel. His own son, a rebel! Henry might be a poor creature, but surely he could never have agreed to that!

The earl was getting desperate. He ordered Bristol to send a fleet of galleys across to Newport and convey his forces from South Wales by sea. The royalists scotched that plan by commandeering other ships at Gloucester and sending them to destroy the Bristol convoy. Foiled, the earl turned inland again, seized Monmouth, but was driven back in an attempt to cross the Wye. For some time he marched to and fro in Breconshire, accomplishing little except to make a bargain with the Welsh prince, Llewellyn, who lent him some infantry. Then, after ranging as far north as Leominster in an effort to break out of his cage, he fell back on his original base at Hereford.

So June passed, and most of July. The Plantagenet leopard prowled watchfully along the eastern bank of the Severn, and the De Montfort lion, old and wary, crouched in Hereford, waiting for a chance to spring. And ordinary men went about their work, carting the hay and watching the corn ripen on their strips. The apples reddened in the Herefordshire orchards, the plums filled out and softened in the Vale of Evesham and around the gray walls of Pershore Abbey, and it was hard to realize that, before summer was out, there must be a harvest of a grimmer kind.

"Arlette!" It was the countess calling from the doorway. Arlette sprang to her feet. "Madam?"

Her hostess sailed into the room, a smile on her lips. "So we are not to have you with us much longer, my dear."

"I—I don't know what you mean—"

"News from Rome, child! Everything is all right.

114

The Earl of Renfield is free to marry you." She took Arlette's hand and laughed. "A splendid match for you! You'll be a countess. Let me see, now—won't you be the youngest countess in England?"

"I don't care," said Arlette in a leaden tone.

"Gracious, child, you must show a little more enthusiasm than that! Modesty is all very well—a young girl shouldn't appear eager—but it is to be a wedding, you know, not a funeral. Renfield will be here tonight. You must have a smile to welcome him."

"Tonight, madam? Here?"

"Yes," said the countess briskly. "Which reminds me, I have a hundred things to see to. Renfield is with Simon—my son, Simon, of course, not the earl."

Arlette licked her dry lips. "Will they stay long?"

"I doubt it. They have to join my husband."

The countess hurried away to give orders to her steward. Arlette flung herself onto the window seat and stared moodily across the battlements to the wavy green distance of Arden. Tears pricked her eyes.

There was no man in the world she wanted to marry, but there must be plenty she could have taken with a good grace, if the king had bidden her. She had never grown up with any hope of choosing for herself. And in her blackest moods at Kenilworth she had often felt that any marriage, almost, would have been better than none. At least it would have meant a kind of escape. You could not be treated as a child once you were married.

But not to the Earl of Renfield! Not even to be the youngest countess in the kingdom. She would never feel like a countess while that other woman was alive, who had borne the title for the past five years. Whatever the Roman lawyers had decided, she would always feel that the earl had deserted one wife to gain the estates of a second.

It came over her suddenly, like the breaking of a wave, that she could not do it. Not for the king himself, not even for the terrifying Earl Simon. Could she brace herself to defy him? Was there any other way out?

It was at that moment, as she huddled miserably in the window recess, staring out unseeingly over the forest, that she made up her mind to run away.

Young Simon's army began streaming into the town during the afternoon. Six or seven thousand men, Arlette heard someone say, more than the number his father had mustered at Hereford. They had made a triumphal march from Sussex, plundering Winchester on the way.

"Between us," Simon boasted to his mother at supper, "we shall do the trick. We shall catch Edward's army and crack it like a nut."

Arlette hated his self-confidence, but, after watching that endless line of banners flowing into Kenilworth, she knew that he had reason. Once the two De Montfort columns were united, Edward would be outnumbered.

"How long will you stay here?" inquired the countess. "Only till the morning?"

"A little longer. I'm expecting a supply column. Father knows I am coming via Kenilworth. He'll be sending word where he wants me to join him."

116

"Well, your chamber is ready."

"Oh, I shall sleep in the town, Mother—with the men. I can keep an eye on them better, there."

After the meal, when the high-table party had retired to the great chamber, the countess swept over to Arlette with the Earl of Renfield smiling at her side.

"This is a busy time to talk of weddings," she began, "but when the gentlemen are so much occupied with other matters, we must catch them when we can."

Arlette did not return their smiles. She looked stonily at the earl. He was a handsome-enough man, she had to admit. Thirty, or thereabouts. A brave rider in tournaments, well-mannered, witty . . . oh, a great many things. But she did not like the calculating look in his gray eyes.

"This match has been talked of for a long time," he told her pleasantly. "But there have been . . . impediments."

"Are there none now, my lord?" she asked, but he took no notice of her sarcasm.

"I have been thinking," he went on, "and the countess here is quite agreeable—since we are to be here for a day or two, and all the practical details have been thrashed out long ago, need we wait?"

"Wait?" she repeated, stunned by the suddenness of it.

"The king is willing. The difficulty has been removed. We could be married here tomorrow morning."

"What do you think of that?" put in the countess warmly.

Arlette was hastily pulling herself together. Outright defiance would put them on their guard. She must pretend. She threw up her head proudly.

"No, madam, it would be too hurried. When I am married I want a proper wedding—not a ceremony rushed through in the chapel here before my lord rides off with the army. I am the king's ward, and I want the king to give me away. And proper clothes, not just anything."

The countess laughed. "She's not really vain," she told Renfield apologetically. "Most girls would say the same."

"After all," added Arlette wickedly. "One is only married *once*. Or should be." The thrust went home to both her hearers.

"Well, there's no more to be said then, at the moment," said the countess quickly, going somewhat red. "There are plenty of other things to see to, without weddings."

"We shall not have to wait long," said Renfield. "There is this rebellion to settle, and then, before the bells have stopped ringing for victory, they can start again for us."

Never, vowed Arlette with a shudder. Making the excuse of a headache, she slipped from the crowded room.

It had better be tonight, she resolved. With the castle in confusion, and the town packed with troops, it might be possible to slip away unnoticed.

14

Margot the Spy

IF ARLETTE HAD NEVER seriously considered running away until now, it was because she had been unable to think of anywhere to run to.

The only home she could remember was the nunnery, far away in the north. And she preferred not to imagine the welcome she would have received from Sister Helena, let alone the prioress, even supposing that she managed the long journey without being recaptured.

She had no lover to run to, or with; only from—if you could count the Earl of Renfield as a lover. In books of romances, or in the Provençal songs they had sung in the queen's chamber at Nottingham, there had always been a knight-errant to rescue damsels in distress. Well, she had languished at Kenilworth for two long years, and not one had appeared. None of the knights she had ever met seemed to have time to be errant; when they were not being called up for military service, they were far too busy on their own manors.

The Lord Edward was the nearest to her ideal, but at the moment he was probably busier than anybody.

Still, she told herself doggedly, he had taken the vows of knighthood and she was sure he would never deliberately break them. "I am not asking him to rescue me, anyhow—though I did once offer to help him when *he* was a prisoner here. I shall rescue myself, but if I can reach his camp and ask for his protection, how can he refuse? If I am not a 'distressed damsel,' I should like to know who is!"

Edward was at Worcester. Thirty-four miles, that was reckoned, from Kenilworth. With a good horse she could cover them in a night. The first half of the journey, as far as Alcester, she had ridden several times during her stay at Kenilworth, and once she had been taken all the way to Worcester itself for a great thanksgiving in the cathedral. So, with the promise of clear moonlight, she thought she could find the road.

Obviously, a disguise was needed. Escaping heroines normally traveled "in the garb of a page." The romances were all agreed on that, just as heroes dressed up as women. With the long ride in front of her, and the countryside alive with armed wanderers, she would be less likely to be stopped if she went as a youth.

Getting the clothes, on short notice, was not so easy. The storytellers never troubled themselves with such practical details. There was no one whom she dared tell of her plan. One small page, Martin—known as Mouse—would cheerfully have died for her. When she was in sight, he was apt to stare at her in a daze of worship. She decided she would have to take advantage of this devotion, but without bringing him into any serious danger.

"Mouse!" she called him softly.

And he sprang up and ran to her. If he had possessed a tail he would clearly have wagged it.

"Will you do something for me, Mouse?"

He looked up at her, swallowing hard. "Yes, Arlette," he breathed, husky with bliss.

"I want some boy's clothes," she whispered. "Just for a joke, you know."

"Of course! But—" His face fell. "Anything of mine would be—" He hesitated. Poor lamb, she thought, stifling a chuckle, he can't bear to admit I could never get into anything of his. Mouse liked to imagine himself as a stalwart youth instead of a small boy of ten.

"I thought something of Peter's," she said quickly, naming one of the senior pages nearly as old as herself, "but I didn't want to ask him. It's—it's part of the joke, you see. It's got to be absolutely secret. Just you and me."

"I see, Arlette." He wagged his head, his happiness restored by being singled out. "I'll get you something."

"Bless you!"

He scuttled away. In five minutes he was back, grinning all over his chubby little face. He had brought hose, shirt, a short garment of tunic length reaching barely to the knee, with a hood, and a cloak to go over everything. "And here's a pair of my own shoes," he added proudly. "Peter's would be like boats on you. I think you could wear mine, though. I have rather large feet for my age, and yours . . ." His voice trailed away in a sigh of rapture. The daintiness of Arlette's feet seemed to leave him speechless.

121

She was glad to find that she could, with a little gentle leverage, get into the shoes. "Thank you, Mouse. I knew I could count on you."

"Of course! I only wish—"

"Listen carefully, Mouse. This is for your own sake as well as mine. Don't tell anybody—ever—that you helped me to get these clothes. Peter might give you a beating."

"All right, Arlette."

"I like you better than anybody at Kenilworth," she said impulsively, and stooped to bestow a hasty kiss on the tip of his snub nose. Leaving him paralyzed by the double bliss of her words and gesture, she ran upstairs to find a quiet corner where she could change unseen. Poor Mouse! Would he shed a few unmanly tears tomorrow morning, when he realized that his adored one had vanished forever? Oh, well, he's young, she consoled herself with the mature philosophy of the middle teens—he'll get over it.

There remained the problem of getting a horse. Should she try to take one she knew, from the castle stables—which would mean riding it through the gateway and risking being caught—or should she slip out into the town on foot, and untether one in the horse lines of the camp?

She decided that the first method, though it had its dangers, would be the better. If she used the second, she would have to ride an unknown beast, probably without a saddle, and most likely tired from a long day on the road. She must simply hope that, with so much coming and going in the castle, she would not be recognized in the dusk. With the town full of friendly troops, the gates still stood wide open and the drawbridge was down, so that she would have no need to trouble the porter to let her out.

It was dark when she went out to the stables; the moon was rising but not yet high enough to clear the battlements, and the passing torches made the rest of the night seem darker still. There was a good deal of noise. Young Simon and his friends were singing and drinking in the hall, and the troops were relaxing after the long marches of the past few days. The ale was flowing freely. A steady murmur came from the town outside, rising sometimes to a crescendo of cheering or drunken song, and even inside the castle walls the warm summer darkness was alive with laughter and hoarse whisperings.

Arlette slipped unchallenged into the stable where her favorite mare was kept. Yes . . . Grise was in her place, turning to whinny softly and nuzzle the hand she knew. That was lucky. She would rather take Grise than any horse in the castle. She was not used to saddling her own mount, nowadays, but she had done it often enough as a child to manage after a few fumblings.

"There," she whispered, when the last strap was buckled. "Now we'll just see if there's anybody about—"

At that moment the doorway was blocked by two vague shapes. Arlette froze where she stood. To her relief, the figures made no move to come inside. She heard a rough voice say:

"No, I won't do it!"

And an answering voice—a woman's, to her surprise—whispered furiously:

"You promised!"

Arlette breathed again. Just a lovers' tiff, she decided. One of the serving girls who had picked up with a man-at-arms and as quickly fallen out with him again.

"I can't help what I promised," said the man in a surly tone.

"But I counted on you—there's no one else—"

"Well, I won't. I value my skin too much."

"Very well, then," said the woman's voice coldly. First one of the blurred figures, and then, a moment later, the other, moved out of the doorway. Arlette waited and then, to be on the safe side, crept out to inspect the courtyard. To her alarm, a stocky little figure was standing motionless a yard or two away. The tip of the moon was appearing above the battlements, and she could make out the glint of an iron cap. It must be the man-at-arms she had just heard.

It was too late to draw back. He turned with a startled sound. His hands went up, and she felt strong fingers at her throat. She tried to cry out, but managed only a strangled sob. The force of the man's attack threw her onto the trampled straw inside the stable, and he fell after her. She struggled wildly, clutching vainly at the smooth leather of his jerkin. He was a small fellow, and no great weight. If only she could throw him off and get to her feet, she could probably hold her own against him.

Suddenly the grip on her throat slackened a little. "How much did you hear, lad?" panted her assailant. Arlette was so amazed that she stopped struggling. For the voice, rough and grim though it sounded, was

124

not the man's she had previously heard, but the girl's.

"I—I'm not a lad," she gasped.

"*What?*" It was the stranger's turn to show surprise. But, though she took her fingers off Arlette's throat, she made no move to let her rise. "Not a lad?"

"No."

"No more you are! What's the game?"

"I might ask *you* that."

"You'd best not. One squeak from you, and, lad or lass, you'll get six inches of this dagger. Who are you working for? Which side? You are a spy?"

"Certainly not."

"What's the meaning o' these clothes, then? And skulking about in the stables, listening to other folks' talk? You talk like a lady. Frenchified. Is it just some lark with your young man?"

"I haven't a young man," said Arlette indignantly. "I am not a spy, and I am not in the least interested in what you were saying to *your* young man—if that's what he was. And now will you kindly get off my stomach?"

"Just a minute, just a minute. Sorry to sound rough, my dear, but I'm risking my neck tonight. Who are you, and what are you up to? I want the truth, mind."

"All right. I am Arlette de la Garde. I'm a ward of King Henry—so you really *will* be risking your neck if you touch me with that dagger of yours. I'm dressed like this, and I'm skulking about in the stables, as you call it, because I'm running away." Briefly she explained the situation.

"Good for you," said the stranger approvingly. She got to her feet and pulled Arlette after her. "Sorry if I gave you a shock, dear, but you gave me one too, I can tell you. So you're going to the Lord Edward at Worcester, are you?"

"I am."

"Would you like to do something for me—and for him?"

"Yes."

"Then take the message that rat wouldn't. There's no one else I can send. I could take it myself, but my orders were to stay with the enemy as long as possible—"

"The enemy? You mean—you—you're spying for the Lord Edward?" stammered Arlette delightedly.

"Sh! Not so loud, lass. Yes, that's it. That's why I'm wearing this gear. Tell the Lord Edward what's happened. Young Simon has between six and seven thousand men. They'll be here for a day or more. Then they'll be moving west to link up with the earl. That's what the Lord Edward ought to know."

"I'll tell him," Arlette promised. Her heart leaped. She would go to Edward not as a distressed damsel, interrupting the serious business of war, but as a bearer of vital news.

"Say Margot sent you," said the strange young woman in the helmet and jerkin. "He'll know the name."

Five minutes later, Arlette rode Grise across the drawbridge. The moon was high now, the lake a shield of polished silver, and the thick-ranked oaks of Arden made a murmurous darkness beyond the gables of the town.

15

The Leopard Springs

HEADING DUE WEST, she had no need to pass through the town. Its noise, and the rosy glare of its watch fires, fell at once behind her: in front stretched the countryside, cool and empty and still.

No sentry challenged her. Even to her unmilitary mind it seemed that young Simon was a little careless. But no doubt he could afford to feel confident, surrounded by so large an army and knowing that the Lord Edward was over thirty miles away, pinned down on the banks of the Severn by the need to hold its crossings against the earl.

How silent were the hamlets she rode through! Not a light winked behind the barred doors and shutters. Were all the people asleep? Or were they quaking in their beds as the dogs barked and the hoofbeats thudded down the lane?

She saw nobody until she reached Alcester. The little town stood at the meeting place of two rivers, and it was impossible to avoid passing down the main street. A watchman stepped out of the shadows and barred her way. He raised a long pike. It flashed silvery blue in the moonlight. She drew rein.

"In the king's name!" His voice was firm but kindly, a mellow Warwickshire voice, not unwelcome after the miles of loneliness. "Where are ye for, sir, this time o' night?"

She had foreseen such a situation. She pitched her own voice as deep as she could. "On the king's business," she said boldly. In ordinary times no one would hinder a king's messenger—the punishment was too severe—and she must gamble on the watchman's behaving with the usual respect. As both sides claimed to be acting in the king's name, it was a safe-enough answer, provided the man did not ask for further details.

He still hesitated, blocking her road. "I suppose that's all right, young man, but it's like this—I've had orders—"

"I'm in a hurry," she interrupted. "You know what it means to hold up the king's messenger?"

"Ay," he said unhappily, "but ye see—"

She must take a chance. "Don't you know this ring?" she demanded haughtily. She thrust out her hand. The gold flashed under his nose. It was no ring in particular, but she counted on the man's ignorance and fear of getting into trouble. The gamble came off.

"Beg pardon, sir, I'm sure!" He raised his head after a mere pretense of inspecting the ring—it would have taken a keen eye to have made out much detail by moonlight. "Can't be too careful, though, in these days. Good night, sir." He fell back, lowering his pike, and she rode on, exultant with relief.

After another mile or two she felt safe enough to halt and give Grise a rest. She sat down on the bank of a friendly-looking brook, which went chuckling through the long grass between two orchards and winking up at the moon. Grise drank, and she drank too. Grise munched some of the grass with long, tearing noises, and Arlette wished ruefully that she had thought to bring some food with her. Then she laughed suddenly. "What a fool I am!" she exclaimed aloud, and stretched her arm above her head. The trees were laden with ripe plums. Their skins were satin smooth, and the beads of dew gleamed like pearls upon them. She ate a great many, and tried to see how many stones she could spit across the brook. How the countess would have disapproved!

There was a limit, though, to the number of plums one could enjoy in the middle of the night. She would have given the rest of the orchard for a bowl of steaming broth and a hunk of the coarsest bread. It was eerie, sitting there under the creaking, whispering boughs. Even the chuckle of the brook developed a sinister note after a time. Now that the worst of the human dangers were behind her, her mind began to run on other perils—on ghosts and evil spirits and the Devil himself. Once an owl startled her. Looking up, she half expected to see a witch sailing over the plum trees astride her broomstick.

"It's time I got astride Grise again," he told herself firmly and jumped to her feet, licking the juice from her fingers. It was comforting to feel the mare nuzzling her as she tightened the girth. Once mounted and trotting down the road, she felt her courage flowing back. Tired she was, and heavy-eyed, but the thought that she had escaped from Kenilworth upheld her.

The short summer night was passing. She was in Worcestershire now. The moon glittered from a cloudless sky, lighting up the countryside for miles. To her left, across the broad valley of the Avon, she could see the sudden hump of Bredon Hill, and even, far beyond it, the dimmer shapes of the Cotswolds. Another ten miles should bring her to Worcester. She yawned. Grise plodded steadily forward. Clop-clop, clop-clop.

She must have sat longer by the brook than she had meant to, for soon, when she glanced over her shoulder, she saw a whitening sky. Cocks crowed. The returning day sent long rosy fingers slanting and splaying above the Cotswold ridge, and she suddenly saw the castle and the cathedral rising from the mist ahead of her.

The Lord Edward's camp was well watched. She was stopped by a mounted patrol before she reached the outskirts of the city. She was beginning to explain herself when a young squire cantered up to inquire what was happening. For a few moments they stared at each other, unable to believe their eyes. She had looked forward to seeing Michael, but she was not prepared for seeing him helmeted, in chain mail that twinkled in the sunrise, hardly a boy any longer but a fighting man. And he had never expected to see her at all, and certainly not in hose, with her dark hair snaking untidily from beneath a page's hood.

"What in heaven's name—" he began.

"I've an urgent message for the Lord Edward," she said proudly.

"You have?"

"From one of his agents at . . . you know where."

"Then I'd better take you to him at once. I'm his squire, now," Michael added casually, but the point was lost upon Arlette.

"At once?" she echoed in dismay. She glanced down, embarrassed, at her legs and raised a distracted hand to fiddle with her tousled hair.

And, with a boy's stupidity, he answered: "Why ever not?"

The Lord Edward could not have received her with more courtesy had she arrived like the Queen of Sheba. A cushioned chair was brought. Bread and wine were set on a low table beside her, the wine warmed and spiced to ward off the effects of the night air. She sipped gratefully from the steaming cup while the Lord Edward, more like a leopard than ever, paced the room and poured out eager questions. Then, when she had told him all she knew, Michael had to escort her to a nearby convent, where she could go straight to bed.

"I'm so sleepy," she yawned, her words muffled against her hand. "There's so much to tell you—and ask you—but it'll have to wait. I'll see you this evening."

"That'll depend," he answered, his eyes bright with excitement. "We might be gone by the time you wake up. This news alters everything!"

But they were not gone as soon as that. The Lord Edward had to do some hard thinking and talk the matter over with Gilbert de Clare and Mortimer. Also, with his forces scattered along the Severn bank to guard each crossing, he needed time to gather them together.

The decision was difficult. Even Michael could see that. They were now between two armies of the enemy. Earl Simon was twenty-seven miles away at Hereford; young Simon was slightly farther off at Kenilworth. If they were given time to link up, the outlook for the royalists was black.

The obvious course was to take on the two armies one at a time, before they could combine. "Tackle the weaker first," said the old campaigners. But which *was* the weaker? The earl's was slightly the smaller in numbers, but with the earl in command it might be more dangerous than his son's.

To attack young Simon would mean the risk of leaving the Severn defense line temporarily unguarded. To march against his father would mean crossing the river—and that could not be done in a moment, with ten thousand men. There was not the faintest hope of surprising the earl after such a maneuver, he was too old a hand. But what about his son? There was no broad river between Worcester and Kenilworth. Arlette had shown that the distance could be covered overnight. What were the chances of a surprise attack at dawn, following a forced march?

No man could tell. Through that Friday night Michael kept waking to hear his master tossing restlessly on his bed, or getting up to walk the room. So much was at stake. . . . If the decision was wrong, it meant defeat and probably the end of their cause.

On Saturday morning a white-faced young giant had come to his decision, for good or ill. The outlying detachments were to be called in during the day. Men and horses were to rest as far as possible. Everyone was to be ready to move by the afternoon.

Their destination was kept a close secret. Michael shared the secret with the leading barons in the royalist army. Kenilworth! It would be amusing to see the place again in such altered circumstances.

It was no less amusing for Arlette. Having made up her own lost sleep, she gave Michael no peace until he got leave for her to ride with the army. Her knowledge of the road and of Kenilworth might be useful, she insisted, and, if the Lord Edward was prepared to use women like Margot, to move disguised among the common soldiers of the enemy, he could hardly object to her coming.

Michael was not too pleased when leave was given. She saw it and demanded: "Don't you want me?"

"Of course," he protested. "But . . ."

"But what?"

"It's no sort of expedition for a girl—a night march—"

"There'd have been no night march, but for me," she retorted. "Considering that I made the journey one way alone, I should think I could manage it with the army."

Michael was silent. All the normal arguments seemed rather foolish under the circumstances. Arlette would be safer with them than if she remained in the weakly guarded town. There was no question of her being able to keep up with the men, since she would be mounted, whereas a large proportion of the army was on foot.

The real reason for his reluctance was something he could hardly put into words. The Lord Edward had insisted that Arlette must stay right in the rear, out of harm's way, when the fighting started—and Michael was afraid that he might be told to look after her, when his rightful place was at his master's side in the front of the battle. Arlette was his friend, he was delighted to see her again, and his admiration for her was greater than ever as the result of her escape from the De Montforts. But a boy's first battle was a tremendous experience, and he needed to give up his whole mind to it, not to be distracted by other thoughts and feelings. For the first time since he had known Arlette, he would have preferred her absence to her company. However, Edward had given his permission, so there was no more to be said.

Saturday morning seemed endless. At last the midday meal was over, and he went off, much too early, to get ready. It was the last day of July, and a torrid sun was beating down upon the Vale of Severn. They were going to swelter, he realized, before darkness brought relief. First there was the quilted tunic to put on under his armor—a heavy garment padded with tow and shreds of cloth, horrible to wear in such weather but absolutely necessary to take the force of any blow landing on his body. Then there were the chausses, or breeches, of soft leather, with rows and rows of overlapping iron rings stitched to them, and the hauberk, or shirt, of similar chain mail. As though this were not enough, there was a linen surcoat to wear over it.

"You'll be the cooler for it," Edward assured him, smiling at the lobsterlike complexion of his squire.

"Cooler, my lord?"

"That's what the Crusaders found in Palestine—they started the fashion for surcoats. If you had the hot sun b-beating straight d-down on the metal, you'd be f-fried!"

At least, Michael thanked heaven, there was no need to wear his helmet until the moment of action. It could hang on his saddle bow, together with his gauntlets. It was some relief to have the fresh air on his face and hands.

He helped Edward to arm, and at five o'clock the order to move off was given. It seemed to Michael a very early start for a journey which Arlette had not begun in the opposite direction until after dark, but Edward had worked out his timetable with care. Long columns of troops, he knew from experience, never traveled as fast as small parties. There were always apt to be hitches. The head of the column might get held up, in which case the others would bunch together behind. Or something might happen to delay the contingents in the rear, so that those in front must wait for them. A man by himself might walk four miles in an hour, but an army would average something between two and three.

Michael did not mind the early start. He was eager to be off. He had never felt prouder than when he rode out of Worcester behind his master, carrying Edward's shield and wearing on both sleeves the red cross of the royalists.

He need not have worried that Arlette's presence would rob him of his proper place as Edward's squire. When they halted for breakfast near Kenilworth, in the haze of an August dawn, one of the advance patrols returned with the spy, Margot, and Arlette was entrusted to her.

"Very good, my lord," said Margot. "But first I've something to tell you. There's a party o' their foragers coming out—you'll not want them running into us and giving the alarm. I can show you a place, though, a little valley like, quite near the camp. Lay an ambush for 'em, my lord, an' they'll ride straight into it!"

It worked out as she had promised. There was a grassy dell, tufted with hawthorns and silvered with the heavy dew. Rabbits were beginning to play, until the first footsteps sent them flashing back into their holes.

Edward gave brief orders. A company of archers, throwing off the weariness of their long march, trotted forward and vanished among the bushes as completely as the rabbits had done. Margot grinned cheerfully and stalked away, leading a reluctant Arlette. Edward posted his knights and turned to Michael. "My helmet," he said briefly.

Michael raised the heavy cylinder of iron in both hands. Edward ducked helpfully, and at once his voice became muffled as it settled on his head. "Gloves . . . thank you. And now my shield." Michael passed it over. "Quiet, now. They're coming."

It was getting light. The sky was blue-gray and scaly, like a mussel shell. The mist, herald of another hot day, lay in white swaths across the ground, cutting off the lower branches of the hawthorns and hiding all but the heads and shoulders of men standing any distance away. Voices, and the tramp of heavy horses, came nearer. The birds overhead still chirred in their usual dawn chorus. Michael peered anxiously through the tiny slits of his helmet, turning his head this way and that, feeling half blind inside his unaccustomed head covering. Then, just as he made out the straggling line of the forage party lumbering across his line of vision, he heard the terrifying sound of a hundred bowstrings twanging together, a hundred arrows thudding and rattling on soft flesh and stubborn iron. "Come on!" roared Edward, and Michael spurred after him. The line of knights poured down the slope like a breaking wave.

There was little-enough fighting, then, or later. The foragers were swamped. Those who had not fallen to the first volley of arrows were cut down or captured within a breathless minute or two. Their horses were seized and handed to the weariest of the infantry.

"And now," cried Edward jovially, "we'll wake up my cousin Simon! Remember, I want him alive."

They burst into Kenilworth just as the sky was crimsoning above the rooftops. The surprise was complete. They thundered down the main street, waving their swords and shouting to the sleepers: "Come out, traitors! Come out and be killed!" Then throwing themselves from their saddles, they began to break down the doors.

Some of Simon's knights were killed or captured in their beds. Others jumped from windows or ran out by back doors, their shirts fluttering around their bare legs; others, stark naked, stayed only to snatch up their clothes in their hands. Few had time to arm and defend themselves.

It was a farce rather than a fight. Some of the noblest lords in England were plopping into the lake like ducks and swimming desperately for the safety of the castle. Young Simon himself had one of the narrowest escapes. Michael saw him, clad only in a pair of drawers, spring into a boat and pole it feverishly across, while the crossbowmen on the bank sent a dozen jets of water leaping in his wake.

Against the castle itself, nothing could be done. The drawbridge was up, the ramparts manned, and they had neither the time nor the engines for a siege. But of the main force, which had been billeted in the town, a few had been killed, many captured, and the rest were scattered and disorganized. The Earl of Oxford was a prisoner, along with twenty other men of note. Thirteen banners were captured and enough horses to mount most of the royalist infantry.

Michael met Arlette at an early dinner, served in one of the bigger houses in the town. She was still gurgling with laughter at the memory of the enemy's panic.

"Did you see the Earl of Renfield—my husband that should have been?" she asked Michael.

"No. Was he taken?"

"Not he! He was last seen running into the forest —he was cut off from escaping to the castle. Running like a deer," she chuckled, "with his hose flapping in his hand, but not daring to stop for a moment to put them on!"

16

A Snare for the Lion

THEY SPENT the whole of that long August day at Kenilworth, resting after their ride. A line of outposts was thrown around the town, and a force was always ready under arms, watchful for any sign of a sortie from the castle, but otherwise the horses grazed peacefully and the men sprawled asleep in the sun. Michael was not the only one who went swimming in the little river that issued from the lake.

Afterward, feeling deliciously cool and clean, he went in search of Arlette. She smiled at him drowsily, like a cat, very pleased with life and herself. She was combing her hair. A merchant's wife had lent her clean clothes.

"Do you think," she said lazily, "that if we shouted across the moat the countess would send me out my own things? Under a flag of truce, I mean."

Michael stared at her and grinned. He liked her impudence. "I somehow doubt that," he said. "But I certainly think you ought to let her know that you're safe."

"Why?"

"Well—I mean—you've lived there for a couple of years—"

"I've hated every minute of it," she interrupted stormily.

"Was that the countess's fault?"

"I suppose not. Oh, she was kind enough in her way. Except when she stopped me from writing to you."

"That doesn't matter now."

"No." Arlette stood up. "All right, Michael. I'll shout across to them if you think I ought to. On one condition." Her eyes twinkled. "They must see you walking along the edge of the water with me. You must allow me a little revenge."

So they walked down to the margin of the lake, and Michael cupped his hands and shouted across. Arlette was evidently recognized by those inside the castle, for there was a bunching of heads along the battlements, some of them female. "You do the talking," Arlette begged him. "I can't shout across that distance. I'd be squawking like a raven."

"All right, leave it to me." And, in the measured tones of a herald making a proclamation, he sent his words ringing across to the listeners on the castle walls. The Lady Arlette de la Garde presented her compliments to the Countess of Leicester, thanked her for her past hospitality, and apologized for her hasty departure. The countess would be glad to know that she was safe and well, and staying with friends.

"You needn't be *so* polite," the girl growled.

Michael was genuinely shocked. "How else could I speak? Just because we are at war with her family, one can't stop behaving like a gentleman."

Whether or not the countess was herself listening, there was no acknowledgment. The only sign was made by a boy, who jumped up into view, waved furiously for a few moments, and then was pulled back by his companions.

"Dear Mouse!" said Arlette.

"Who's Mouse?"

"He's one of the pages. Very sweet."

"How old?" asked Michael suspiciously.

She could not resist the temptation. "Oh, not quite as old as you," she said lightly. "Though he *seems* older. In some ways." Then, having enjoyed his expression for as long as seemed safe, she caught his sleeve as they turned away from the lake. "Not really, Michael. I was joking. He's the little one who got me the clothes to escape in."

Michael was glad that just then they came face to face with his master. Edward stared down at Arlette in surprise.

"Are you s-still here, my dear?"

"Where else should I be, my lord?"

"I th-thought you would be on your way to Gloucester by now. The prisoners are going there under escort. It s-seemed a good idea for you to go with them. I sent a messenger to tell you, but I s-suppose he could not find you. Oh, well, you had better stay with us a little longer, till we can decide what to do with you."

"Thank you, my lord." Arlette could be very meek when it seemed advisable. Privately, she had decided to stay with the army as long as she could.

She had not bargained for another night ride, but she did not breathe a word of complaint when the order came around to be ready after dusk. She had at-

141

tached herself to the army, and she knew she must bear the same hardships as the others. They could do nothing more for the present against young Simon, secure inside the island fortress, and his father, prowling dangerously on the western bank of the Severn, must not be neglected any longer.

So the thirty-four miles back to Worcester were doggedly retraced that night and the following morning. But when, on the afternoon of August 2, they rode triumphantly into the city, bad news awaited them.

Their chief enemy had not been idle. His scouts had discovered that the river crossings were no longer fully guarded. He had collected a number of boats at Kempsey, only four miles downstream from Worcester, and had been ferrying his troops across most of the day. By now the bulk of his army was over the obstacle that had held him up for so long.

Edward's face darkened as he listened to the report. He glanced at the travel-stained faces around him, at the drooping heads of the horses. He knew that the earl should have been attacked hours ago, while his army was still perilously divided east and west of the river. It was too late now. He could not ask his exhausted troops to cover another four miles and fight a fresh army, commanded by the most experienced general alive.

"It must be tomorrow," he said grimly.

But when they awoke, early next day, the earl had already disappeared. He had marched off before dawn, taking the road to Evesham. Edward conferred hurriedly with Mortimer and the De Clares. There was much talk of roads and bridges and distances, much drawing of sketch-maps. Michael, in the background, listened eagerly.

"What is the old man's game?" queried Mortimer. "He must know by now that his son is at Kenilworth —though he can hardly know yet that we've been there too! You'd expect him to make for Kenilworth by the quickest road, through Alcester—"

"Passing under our noses here in Worcester?" Edward interrupted scornfully. "He's not such a f-fool."

"Suppose he makes straight for London?" suggested Gilbert de Clare.

"He might. London's his great source of strength."

"If it's London," said Mortimer nervously, "we shall never catch up with him. And once he gets there . . ." He left the sentence unfinished. There was silence in the room. Everyone knew how serious it would be. In a few hours the whole position had changed for the worse. The easy triumph at Kenilworth was a mere memory. Once more they were faced with grim odds.

Edward considered for a few moments, then gave his opinion. Nothing was certain. They must guess what was most probable from what they knew of the earl. Was it likely that the victor of Lewes would run for London, without a fight, like a rat making for its hole? No. He would try to join forces with young Simon and then turn on his enemies; no rat, but an old lion at bay.

"A messenger, my lord!" announced Michael from the doorway.

"S-send him in."

A sweating scout marched in and saluted. "I've ridden from Pershore, my lord—"

"Yes?"

"Earl Simon's crossing the bridge over the Avon there. I watched them with my own eyes."

"Pershore . . . then he's keeping on for Evesham. Halfway there by now."

"He'll not get farther tonight, my lord. It's a narrow bridge."

"Yes . . . like a bottleneck. . . . It's bunching them up, I suppose?" Edward spoke decisively. At such moments his stammer disappeared. He turned to the sketch he had previously drawn on a piece of parchment. "You're right. He'll get no farther than Evesham tonight. But what about tomorrow? He may go straight on for London. If he does, we can't stop him. But I think he won't. I think he'll tell young Simon to meet him. And young Simon will have got over his knock by now."

"They mustn't meet, my lord," said Mortimer.

"No." Edward frowned at his sketch and did some silent calculations in his head. "We must throw ourselves between them, stop them from joining at all costs. Once the Kenilworth troops come under the earl's banner, they'll get back their spirit, they'll be dangerous again. . . . Let me see." He scratched his head. "It doesn't make it any easier," he grumbled, "that there are two ways they might come from Kenilworth. There's the Alcester route, and there's another from Stratford, through Cleeve Prior and Offenham. Simon might fancy that more," he chuckled, "because it would give him the Avon to shield his right flank all the way. He may not want any more unpleasant surprises from us."

144

"We can't be sure," Gilbert de Clare objected.

"That's what I said before. Nothing is certain. But"
—Edward laid his long forefinger on the lines he had
drawn—"if we cut the first road *here*, just south of
Alcester, we can push some of our men across the
ford at Cleeve. That will put us astride the river, one
foot on each road. We'll block him for sure, then, if
he comes at all."

Mortimer pursed his lips. "People who straddle
their feet too wide apart are easily knocked off their
balance," he said gloomily.

"We must take that risk." Edward faced his two
allies squarely. He knew that without their agreement he was powerless; their own contingents made
up too large a part of his army. They, on the other
hand, knew that without the king's son as leader they
were little more than desperate rebels against the
De Montfort regime. They had come so far and there
was no turning back. In the fifteen months since
Lewes a change had come over the scene. Everything was bitter and grim. If Earl Simon beat them
he would show little mercy—least of all to those who,
like the De Clares, had changed sides.

"Will you have your men ready to march at dusk?"
Edward asked them.

"Another night march?" Mortimer knitted his
brows. "It will be the third in four days."

"It's the only way of getting there in time," pointed
out Gilbert de Clare.

The conference broke up. Edward saw his allies
to the door and then turned, smiling down at Michael. "Get some sleep, boy—you'll need it. But first

take a message to the prioress. The Lady Arlette is to s-stay in the convent tonight, if it m-means locking her in a cell. That is a royal command."

Michael saw from his face that he was serious, despite his kindly tone, and he carried the order willingly enough. There would be no place for girls in tomorrow's business. It would be no laughing matter, as Kenilworth had been.

Once more there was the slack afternoon: sleep that would not come, just because it would be so desperately wanted later; then the looking to horses and arms, the methodical greasing of bowstrings and sharpening of swords, the clang of blacksmiths' hammers, the hiss of cooling iron; supper, unusually late, in the lengthening sunbeams of evening; then the dressing and harnessing, and, as the sun went down in angry crimson behind the western hills, the slow uncoiling of the army's long columns, creeping snakelike under its banners toward the darkening east. . . .

They reached the first road at Dunnington, three miles south of Alcester, before it was light. Scouts, ranging far to north and south, reported no signs of movement from either direction. The night seemed empty apart from themselves. They were here within seven miles of the earl's army at Evesham. Suppose he was planning another early start?

"At least he can't be here for a little while," said Edward. "We have time to try the other road."

It was agreed that De Clare should wheel his division to the right, straight down the road to Evesham, while Edward and Mortimer pushed on across the Avon. The word was passed down the halted column. They began to move on again. De Clare's men peeled off smoothly into the darkness, the rest went trampling down the hill to the river. Suddenly Michael was aware of the black water rippling in front of them. A scout called reassuringly, and the leading riders splashed into the shallows. For all their efforts to keep quiet, Michael felt that the noise must have been heard for miles.

The sky was still dark when they struck the road at Cleeve Prior. And still there was no sign of the enemy coming either way. Michael began to have a horrible fear that Edward had guessed wrong, that they had marched through the night for nothing, and that somehow the earl had tricked them again. Suppose he was even now vanishing along the London road?

"Not yet," Edward reassured him when he ventured to speak his fear. He explained why, if Simon had spent the night in Evesham, it could not be so. The town lay inside a horseshoe bend of the Avon. To start for London he must get out of the horseshoe by crossing Bengeworth Bridge. And, with perhaps six thousand men, that would take time. "He should have got out of the horseshoe last night, before he camped. Now it may be too late."

They wheeled southward along the road to Evesham, parallel with De Clare's men marching along the ridge on the far side of the river. There were now two columns advancing along the roads which young Simon might have used from Kenilworth. If the earl was really expecting his son, he would have an unwelcome surprise. It needed no experience of warfare to tell Michael that.

147

They rode for several miles farther. Dawn was breaking when they reached the village of Offenham. They could see the little town of Evesham not far away across the placid white river. The tower of the abbey stood out against the sallow sky. Edward rose in his stirrups and scanned the London road. There was no sign of movement on all its length, as far as the eye could reach.

He turned to Mortimer. "Will you carry on, this side of the river, and block their way out of the town across the Bengeworth Bridge?" He waved his hand toward another track, which curved away to Offenham Bridge and thence climbed the steep ridge to join the Alcester road. "I'll take my own division and join Gilbert up there. I think we are in luck. Who would have thought so wily an old lion would have fallen into such a snare?"

17

Murder at Evesham

THERE WAS NO FRESHNESS in the morning air. Michael felt stifled under his padded jerkin and heavy mail. Massive clouds blotted out the sunrise, so that the eastern sky, instead of being rose and gold, had the sullen tint of bronze. He was aware of a dull headache, which at first he thought was due to lack of sleep. Then he realized that it was the feeling he always had before a thunderstorm. The heat wave was about to break.

"Come with me," said Edward. "I must ride forward and speak to the Earl of Gloucester." He turned to one of his knights. "Lead on across the bridge and up the hill, after us. Furl our banners until the word is given. Show the ones we captured at Kenilworth."

"The—the captured ones, my lord?"

"Yes, yes. De Montfort won't have seen the Earl of Gloucester's column yet—the crest of the hill hides them—but he'll see you as you come up the slope. The banners may puzzle him. He'll think it's his son from Kenilworth."

"Very good, my lord." The knight rode down the halted column, passing on the order.

Edward spurred forward with Michael and a cluster of knights at his heels. They crossed Offenham Bridge and walked their horses up the stiff incline beyond. The lane was crowded with dismounted men of Gloucester's division, who sprang up and saluted when they recognized Edward. "His lordship is up there, by the crossroads," said one, pointing up the hill.

The two young De Clares were snatching a hurried breakfast under a thorn tree, where the lane from Offenham cut across the main Alcester-Evesham road. Edward swung his long limbs from the saddle, accepted a cup of wine, and began to talk quickly, munching a piece of bread as he did so.

The position was plain. Their combined forces would, in a matter of minutes, be gathered in the open end of the horseshoe formed by the curve of the Avon. The enemy was trapped. To left and right lay the river, and behind them too, with only the narrow outlet of Bengeworth Bridge. Very soon even that bolt hole would be stopped by Mortimer. In front was the Alcester road, climbing a steepish hill from the town. And on the top of that hill, just hidden from them beyond the skyline, Gloucester's division was already marshaling for battle and Edward's moving up to join it.

From riverbank to riverbank, the open end of the horseshoe was well over a mile wide. Perhaps two thousand yards. With less than ten thousand men, they could not close the whole gap, unless they made the battle line dangerously thin.

"We'll hold the high ground in the middle," Edward decided. "If they try to slip by on either flank, we can always charge down the slope and push them into the water."

Gilbert de Clare took the right wing. He was to hold the main road itself and everything to the right of it. Those of his men who were on the left were quickly mustered and marched over to strengthen their comrades. Edward's division took over their frontage as, still under their captured banners, they moved up the lane from Offenham Bridge.

"Remember," he emphasized, "the earl and his sons are to be taken prisoner, if possible."

"It may be difficult," said Gilbert. "They're fighters. And our men have got their blood up."

"We must do our best. And remember, too, my father is somewhere among them. He must be found and rescued at the first opportunity."

"Of course."

Michael felt that Gilbert might have spoken with more conviction. Young though he was, Michael had learned something of politics and statecraft in these past two years, and he knew that men's words did not always match their thoughts. He could believe in Edward's own stern sincerity, but these barons were different. Loud in their loyalty to King Henry, they might not be unduly sad if the old man did not live to reign over them again. Young Edward would suit them much better.

A knight galloped up to report that there were signs of activity in the town. Trumpets had been heard, calling the men from their billets. Horsemen were mustering in front of the last houses, at the foot of the hill.

"Then we had best be in our places," said Edward.

"Au 'voir, Gilbert. Au 'voir, Thomas." He swung himself into the saddle and trotted back to join his own men. A cheer ran along the line as his face, still unhelmeted, was recognized.

It was not until nine o'clock that Earl Simon marched out. He had delayed, it was said later, so that Mass could be celebrated before starting. He knew, before then, that he had been deceived by the captured banners that had been sighted mounting the flank of the hill. Where *was* his son? He had sent word to him at Kenilworth, but he had not arrived. For a short time his hopes had been raised by the news of a column marching along the opposite bank of the Avon, and wheeling around as though to enter the town by Bengeworth Bridge. Now those hopes were dashed. He knew that it was a royalist column, led by Roger Mortimer. There was just one thing to do: break out, by a smashing blow, along the Alcester road, and then with luck make for the safety of Kenilworth.

A royalist watcher on the brow of the hill waved back the signal that the earl was on the move. Edward turned to Michael. "My helmet, please."

"Here, my lord."

"And my shield."

Michael passed it over and put on his own helmet. His headache was now acute. His nerves were on edge, he felt as taut as a bowstring. When the earl's trumpets all brayed out together, he quivered in his seat. His horse plunged restlessly under him.

Over the crest, under the lowering sky, the earl's army rolled into view. Edward let out an exclama-

152

tion of surprise. He had expected the usual battle line, spread across the open fields like his own. But Earl Simon was coming forward with a formation he had never seen before—a narrow-fronted, dense-packed column, no more than a couple of hundred yards wide, if that.

On they came in their thousands, with the white cross of their party on their breasts. In the front rank, sixty or seventy knights riding knee to knee. Behind them, rank after rank, the rest of the mounted men. Then the English infantry, and, last of all, the Welsh—a terrifying mass of iron-clad flesh, bearing down in all its weight upon the thin-stretched line of the royalists.

"Sound our trumpets!" ordered Edward, and the brazen chorus sang out defiance to the advancing column. De Montfort's knights broke into a trot, then a canter. . . . The gap between the armies, six hundred yards at their first sight of each other, narrowed rapidly as the hill rumbled under the drumming hooves. Michael licked his lips and shifted his grip on his sword hilt. Now De Montfort's horsemen were galloping—they were launching their charge at De Clare's left wing, just on the far side of the road. The close air throbbed with the twang of bowstrings. Arrows hailed and rattled. Still the column thundered on. Who could stand against it?

Michael could not help blinking as the two armies crashed together. Through the narrow slits of his helmet he saw that De Clare's line had bent and broken . . . the white crosses of De Montfort were in among the red crosses of the royalists. He could see the long swords rising and falling like flails. Yard by yard the earl's knights were gnawing their way through the men opposed to them.

Edward glanced around and brandished his sword overhead. "Come on!" he bellowed with a sweeping gesture. He rode forward with his picked followers. Michael went just behind him, in the second rank. The whole left half of the royalist line began to wheel, pivoting on the crossroads, and charged in upon the flank of the earl's column.

At first the ground was more or less level. It was easy riding, for it was cultivated land, without trees or brambles, and it was sunbaked firm. But on the far side of the enemy it began to slope steeply toward the river. There was a little stream, too, making its own ravine down to the Avon. Part of the column was rolled headlong into this dip as Edward's men crashed in from the flank.

Someone struck at Michael. The blow glanced painfully but harmlessly from his hauberk. He lashed out instinctively, and missed completely, but it did not matter, since his horse had carried him on. Edward was in front, striking right and left as though possessed of a demon. It was the whirlwind fury of it all which took Michael's breath away—used, as he was, only to the more deliberate actions of drill and exercise. Now, for the first time in his life—Kenilworth had scarcely counted—he was seeing men who were not fencing but striking to kill. And men were dying all around him.

Another blow landed on his helmet. His head sang, he was blinded for a moment, and he rocked in his saddle. As he recovered himself, he saw one of the wild Welsh foot soldiers diving under his horse, dagger in hand. Desperately he struck downward, just in time. The Welshman sprawled and disappeared from view. Michael's horse plunged, but went on again, untouched.

The movement of the two armies had slowed down. They rocked together, like two wrestlers. Both royalist wings had come inward, enfolding the earl's column and squeezing it in a death grip. Their superior numbers began to tell.

Michael's impressions were confused. His eye slits narrowed his view to a jumbled picture of hacking, slashing men, some with white crosses, others with red. He had only two interests for the time being— to keep as close as possible to his master, and to come through the battle alive. In his efforts to do both, he fought better than he realized. Even so, toward the end of the two-hour struggle, a rush of men swept between him and Edward, and he was unable to find him again at once.

Who was winning?

He had no means of telling. He did not know that by now the earl's army had been rolled up into a ball and surrounded, that fugitives were being slaughtered in hundreds as they fled down the hill to Offenham Bridge, and that the earl's Welsh allies were drowning in herds as they leaped despairingly into the Avon. He did not know that the earl himself was dead, and Henry de Montfort, and that his other son, Guy, had been picked up badly wounded and saved at Edward's command.

But where was the captive king?

Out of the crowd, almost under Michael's horse, reeled a figure in plain armor, his face hidden by his helmet, bleeding from a stray arrow. He was unarmed. He wore the cross of neither party.

"Who are you, sir?" Michael demanded, lowering his sword. And in a quavering voice he remembered came the answer:

"I am Henry of Winchester—your king!"

At that moment it was as though the sky cracked across. Lightning leaped up and down the horizon, thunder crashed and rolled across the Vale of Evesham, and, though it was nearly noon, it became so dark that the monks in the abbey could not see to read their scriptures. Another monk, Robert of Gloucester, keeping the chronicle of that other abbey thirty miles away, laid down his quill until the daylight would return. It was he, some time after, who recorded the events of that morning and summed them up in the words: "Such was the murder of Evesham, for battle it was not."

And so ended the long struggle of which men spoke afterward as the Barons' War.

The victors dined late that day in Evesham. Michael, standing at the table, carving for his master and keeping his cup refilled, was almost dead with exhaustion. Edward seemed unaware of his squire's existence. He took his meat and wine mechanically, talking all the time—to his father, to the triumphant lords along the table, and to the messengers who kept tiptoeing up with their whispered reports. But when at last he stood up and pushed back his chair, he smiled suddenly and clapped Michael on the shoulder.

"You fought well, my boy!"

Michael swayed. He felt sick and faint. "You were always in front of me, my lord," he murmured, forcing a smile.

"But there were others who noticed, and told me."

King Henry moved forward to his son's elbow. "He saved me from being trampled underfoot," he said.

"What do you think, Michael? You have not been my squire for long, but it has been a night-and-day affair. Have you won your spurs?" Edward looked down with kindly eyes. "Are you ready for knighthood?"

Michael gasped. Knighthood came in various ways, but to receive it on the field of battle was the highest possible honor. But another thought came to him, and he put the offer from him. "Forgive me, my lord," he stammered in a low voice. "Later—if you think I deserve it—but not today, not at Evesham. You once told me about the day you were knighted in Spain. You said it was a day one should always remember."

"Indeed, yes."

"There are some things I don't want to remember about today. Things that don't go with—with chivalry. Do you understand, my lord?"

A shadow passed across Edward's face. "I think I do," he murmured.

They were both thinking of the savage butchery on that hilltop above the town. The royalist casualties had been heavy enough, but nothing compared with those of the enemy. Four thousand of the earl's army had been killed, including eighteen barons and a hundred and sixty knights. Michael never forgot the look on Edward's face when he heard of Henry de Montfort's death. But there had been worse things.

De Clare's men had stripped the earl's body and hacked it in pieces. The head had been set on a lance point and sent off as a gift to the wife of his old enemy, Roger Mortimer. Young Simon, arriving too late at the head of his Kenilworth army, had seen the horrid sight from a distance, before he turned to retreat along the road by which he had come.

Such sickening barbarities were none of Edward's ordering, but they had happened. Michael would never be able to blot them from his memory as long as he lived, but at least they need not be connected with the day of his knighthood.

A page came running up and bowed to the king. "If it please your grace—"

"Yes, boy?"

"A young lady has arrived from Worcester—she says she is your ward. Arlette de la Garde, my liege."

"Of course, I remember. A pretty girl, but rather a handful. We must get her married."

Edward looked up from a list of names that had just been handed to him. He turned again to Michael. "There is news of interest to you here, my lord."

My lord? Michael gaped. His head was spinning. He clutched the edge of the table for support.

"Lord Sleddale's name is here among those killed on the rebel side, which saves you the trouble of continuing your lawsuit. There was no other claimant, I think. When the clerks have sorted out the details, you will be Lord Grevel."

Michael began to stammer his thanks, but Edward cut him short. "It is no royal favor," he pointed out, "only your right." Then he smiled again, putting off his sternness. "The favor is still to come. You have earned it. If you will not have knighthood, what is it to be?"

At that moment Michael saw Arlette coming down the hall. What had been a hopeless fancy when he was simple Michael Vallier had suddenly become splendidly possible for the new Lord Grevel. He looked up at Edward. "May I tell you tomorrow, my lord? There—there is someone else I shall have to consult."

So peace returned to the land. Young Simon shut himself up in Kenilworth Castle, and there was a six months' siege with much use of giant catapults and other engines, but in the end terms were made and the garrison marched out with all the honors of war. Simon and his brother Guy went into exile abroad; their mother, the widowed countess, entered a convent.

King Henry ruled for another seven years, but from Evesham onward it was really the firm hand of Edward that guided the state, bringing order and law to England, and the end of civil strife. No baron, however proud, ventured to cross swords with Edward. Things were so settled that in 1270 he was able to go on a Crusade, and he was still abroad, two years later, when the news reached him that his father had died and that he was now King Edward I.

Michael did not go with him to the Holy Land. Loyal and trustworthy men were needed at home to carry on the government in his absence, and by then the young Lord Grevel was becoming well known as someone with a bright future at court. His